NO WARNING

Skye Fargo sensed rather than saw danger, and pressed himself against a building. An instant later gunfire speared at him. Two horsemen stormed down the alley in single file, their bullets shattering wood.

Fargo fired twice at the first one, knocking him off his horse as if he'd been hit with a heavy club. The man fell under the chopping hoofs of the second horse, screaming. The other rider fired, and Fargo felt the breath of a bullet. The would-be killer galloped on with raking spurs, out of the passageway and away into the night.

Fargo looked down at the fallen gunman, who was panting curses, twitching feebly on the ground.

"You came all this way to die in an alley," Fargo said softly. "You're a damn idiot, friend."

Then Fargo reloaded his gun and headed out to teach the dying man's pals the same hard lesson the same hard way. . . .

RIDE THE WILD TRAIL

THE TRAILSMAN 74

WHITE HELL

by

Jon Sharpe

A SIGNET BOOK

NEW AMERICAN LIBRARY

PUBLISHER'S NOTE

This book is a work of fiction. Names, characters, places, and incidents either are the product of the author's imagination or are used fictitiously, and any resemblance to actual persons, living or dead, events, or locales is entirely coincidental.

Copyright © 1988 by Jon Sharpe

The first chapter in this book previously appeared in *Santa Fe Slaughter*, the seventy-third book in this series.

SIGNET TRADEMARK REG. U.S. PAT. OFF. AND FOREIGN COUNTRIES
REGISTERED TRADEMARK—MARCA REGISTRADA
HECHO EN CHICAGO. U.S.A.

SIGNET, SIGNET CLASSIC, MENTOR, ONYX, PLUME, MERIDIAN
and NAL BOOKS are published by NAL PENGUIN INC.,
1633 Broadway, New York, New York 10019

First Printing, February, 1988

1 2 3 4 5 6 7 8 9

PRINTED IN THE UNITED STATES OF AMERICA

The Trailsman

Beginnings . . . they bend the tree and they mark the man. Skye Fargo was born when he was eighteen. Terror was his midwife, vengeance his first cry. Killing spawned Skye Fargo, ruthless, cold-blooded murder. Out of the acrid smoke of gunpowder still hanging in the air, he rose, cried out a promise never forgotten.

The Trailsman they began to call him all across the West: searcher, scout, hunter, the man who could see where others only looked, his skills for hire but not his soul, the man who lived each day to the fullest, yet trailed each tomorrow. Skye Fargo, the Trailsman, the seeker who could take the wildness of a land and the wanting of a woman and make them his own.

Winter, 1860–61. The Clearwater Mountain country of eastern Washington Territory, where prospectors gambled their lives against cunning savagery and the raw, whirling fury of icy storms.

1

The weather was still as dry and cold as a witch's tit when Fargo reached the end of the Lolo Trail.

Every day of the past week had been overcast, cold, and dry—to Fargo's great relief. He'd set out from Missoula, gambling he could ride the Lolo Trail from the east side of the Bitterroot Range to the west edge of the Clearwater Mountains before the weather broke all to hell. For two hundred miles Fargo had been bucking towering snowdrifts, deep-numbing freezes, and threatening storms, with occasional sleet flurries and wind-chilling howlers breaking through the frigid calm. Following the ancient Indian path along the ridge of the Lochsa River, he had come down out of the heights to the fertile Weippe Prairie region and the western end of the Lolo Trail.

From here he angled northwesterly, paralleling the Middle Fork of the Clearwater on its course to the Snake. To an Easterner, this stony foothill country could seem bleak, hostile to life, but the Weippe Prairie was a winter-grazing range for hordes of livestock, and thick matts of gray, blue-tinged buckgrass could be seen through the snow.

Fargo sighted a line cabin late that afternoon and another the following day; along toward early sundown of that second day, he noticed that the wind was changing. It had been blowing fitfully in from the south, but now it shifted, became steady, and when Fargo looked toward the "weather pot" in the northwest where this new wind originated, he saw that a silvery haze hung there.

The haze gathered bulk by the moment, rising higher and higher, till it caught up the sun and quenched it. Now it came scudding forward, high overhead, blotting out the sky, swooping low to obliterate distant stands of timber. It began to moan, and soon it was laden with small, compact pellets of snow.

Fargo dug heels into the flanks of his Ovaro, and glanced over his shoulder at his trailing packhorse, a bald-faced dun gelding. The wind was developing into gale proportions when he came upon a little hog wallow of a mining camp called Orofino. While passing through, he paused long enough to draw on his fleece-lined mackinaw, his glance sweeping the squalor. Typical of eastern Oregon and Washington Territory camps, Orofino was mostly tents, luminous structures dappled with grotesque shadows and, at the moment, straining at their guy ropes to blow away in the wind. Turning up his collar, Fargo tucked his sleeves into the flaring cuffs of gauntlet gloves, then shoved off. Vaguely he recalled having heard that Orofino was roughly three dozen miles from Lewiston, the closest hope of a hot bath and hotel bed.

The flakes of snow were larger now, and they drove past Fargo in great swarms, like stampeding white butterflies. Soon he was surrounded by gray darkness, and the cold was pressing in with chilling ferocity.

Suddenly the packhorse floundered, jerking on the lead rope, and Fargo turned, leaning to look behind him. The combination of the packhorse yanking and Fargo leaning was enough to force the Ovaro to lurch off balance, and before he could recover, his mount had slipped out from under him.

Fargo missed his grab for the horn, went spinning across the Ovaro's neck, then rolled with fierce energy when he struck the loose snow because he feared the horse was coming on over. There was a great deal of sliding and pawing and fancy hoofwork, but the Ovaro managed to regain its footing. Instead Fargo heard the snow-muffled thud as the dun gelding landed, and then its panicky scream that told of a snapped leg.

In that initial moment of turmoil, Fargo didn't hear the shooting. He saw the dim shape of the struggling packhorse rear almost on top of him and wrench aside as if hit, then go down again, sprawling. Snow spouted up against his face. He saw, then, the wicked flicker of rifle muzzles, heard the blast of gunpowder. He scrambled to his feet, crouching.

The Ovaro was still tromping dangerously, but it was a case of gambling or being shot like a grazing buck. Fargo went after his Sharps rifle in the saddle scabbard, tearing it free with both hands. A skating foreleg jabbed his ribs, almost knocking him flat. He stopped himself with one knee, loaded and capped the Sharps, and took aim. There were two guns pitching lead out of the dark gloom of the timber that flanked the trail. One of the bullets slammed Fargo's hat sideways on his head. He shot at the flash, rechambered, shot again, then darted for the timber, not about to make a permanent target of himself.

There was only darkness where one of the guns had been firing.

Fargo heard a man's grunting curse, then the crunch of boots running in the snow. He leaped after, straight into the timber. Horses circled there, stamping fretfully in the snow. Cold saddle leather strained protestingly. With only the sounds to guide him, Fargo triggered two more bullets. One thudded into a tree; the other must have been close or a hit, for at once the invisible horse and rider went crashing wildly off through the underbrush.

Gradually the racket faded in the hissing rush of the snow. If Fargo was to have a look at the tracks, there was no time to lose. By the light of sulfur matches struck inside his coat, he headed for the spot where the horses had been standing.

Halfway there, a huddled shape loomed against the white snow. Fargo rolled the man over—he had a straggling red beard and had been shot through the face. Thirty feet farther along the mounts had been tied. One was still there. Fargo ignored it for the while. Shielding the square match with a cupped hand, he studied for signs of the ambusher who had escaped.

He found a good track where overhead branches had kept off the snow. All four shoes were worn, the toes of the hind pair being almost smooth; the off front hoof toed in slightly—at some time or other that leg had been badly bruised.

Lighting matches at intervals, Fargo pushed some two dozen paces along the track where the rider had plowed frantically through the brush. All he found was a strip of dirty canvas, some six inches long and two wide, impaled on the daggerlike end of a broken branch. Canvas storm coats were not uncommon. This strip had come from a sleeve perhaps as the arm slashed down with a quirt or the reins. He tucked it into his pocket and went back to the trail.

The packhorse's near foreleg had been broken just below the knee. Fargo would've had to shoot the poor animal, but the ambushers had already seen to that; the dun gelding was dead. It took most of half an hour to free his pack and rig it on the dead ambusher's horse, a hock-torn dapple mare.

He had been too busy for emotion, but after he was riding again, anger began to build within him. He'd been through trail trouble on his last job ten days ago—bringing an orphan from Omaha to her grandparents in Missoula—but none since then. He wasn't on the prod or after anyone; he was heading to find work as a scout at Fort Walla Walla, or as an Oregon Trail wagon guide out of The Dalles, or whatever might crop up in Portland. And he wasn't carrying anything valuable, just regular foodstuffs and winter gear, and hadn't really needed the packhorse, except as a handy backup when mountaineering in dead of winter. There was no reason for him to have been attacked out here. And if those two bushwhackers hadn't been after him personally, they must've been the hungriest damn bandits in existence to have lain in wait for victims during a blizzard.

Bullshit. There had to be more to it than chance robbery.

Nothing could live long in the full stride of the storm, which was still rising. Snow raged, howling out of the night, whipping his face raw, and driving cold through to his bones. Hustled along by it, the weary Ovaro wandered off course. Fargo had given his mount its head, and was sitting forward in the saddle, hoping that the horse would take him to some draw where they could take shelter.

Abruptly his big black-and-white pinto halted dead in its tracks. Peering ahead, Fargo saw a bunch of steers, which had evidently drifted before the blizzard till they struck a fence line. Now they sullenly awaited whatever came. Some were already down.

Fargo slid out of the saddle and stumbled forward. He could just make out the dark bulk of the individual steers, but his groping fingers traced a brand on left shoulder and flank.

"Star–bar," he muttered. "That's a new one on me."

Fighting his way back to the packhorse, which stood with drooping head, Fargo fished out a new hempen lariat he'd bought in Missoula. Tying one end to the fence and snubbing the other end to his saddle horn, he spurred his Ovaro and wrenched the rails down between two posts. Then, recoiling his rope and tying it on his cantle, he began rousting the steers. After he had them all lumbering through the gap in the fence, he got back into his saddle and again gave the horse its head.

It must have been half an hour later, although Fargo had lost any definite idea of time, that his horse topped a ridge and came quartering down into a valley and again halted. There was some kind of human shelter facing them over there. At first Fargo thought it was a cabin. Then he saw that it was a dugout built into the sloping face of a gully wall.

He didn't stop to pound on the door. It opened

easily to his push and the shove of the wind, and he stumbled into an unlighted room. The air in here was warm, at least in contrast to what he had just been through. Shutting the door, he struck a match and saw a lantern hanging on a peg driven into one sod wall. There were no windows. A rusty cookstove, a homemade chair and table, and a rough bunk covered with blankets and hides made up the spartan furnishings. Whoever owned the dugout had been away from home for some while, judging by the dust and cobwebs.

The Ovaro was pawing at the door. Fargo saw that he couldn't get either horse through the low doorway. He went outside and, with his gloved hands, groped till he found one end of a tight-stretched wire about shoulder-high. Trailing the wire with his left hand, he led the horses through the raging storm. The wind striking them from one side made both horses and man stumble. But the other end of the wire was pegged, as Fargo had guessed, to the front of a second and larger dugout. Blizzard wires were common and necessary in this part of the hills.

Leading the horses inside, he glanced around, smelling the familiar stable odors of saddle leather and horse piss. He couldn't make out much in the shrouded dimness other than a couple of horse stalls along one wall. The stalls were erected out of old, junked sections of galvanized iron roofing, and in the nearer stall was a chestnut mare. Beside the stall, where the frozen ground was relatively cleaner, set a Greeley pack saddle, gear, and a middling full pack—not unlike his own outfit, Fargo reckoned. There was also a pair of bulging leather saddlebags that fit a different rig, which wasn't here that he could see.

He removed his riding gear and pack, and was halfway back to the dugout when he heard an eerie, wind-driven voice.

It wasn't the bawl of a steer, as Fargo, in the first moment, had hoped. It was a man's voice, desperate and exhausted.

2

Fargo tried to shout back, but the wind filled his mouth with snow.

It then dawned on him that he could use the blizzard itself to lead him back to the dugout or at least to this tight-stretched wire, once he had located the stranger. All he would have to do was keep the wind squarely on his back.

This was the first time he had faced into the wind. With one gigantic blow it knocked the breath out of him. He fought forward, body bent, lungs struggling. The cry came again, closer this time.

A deeply splotched paint stood with bowed head, and under it Fargo found the fallen victim of the storm. Snow-encrusted, moving feebly, the man shuddered and collapsed unconscious when Fargo tried to help him up. Fargo draped the poor devil across the horse and together they lunged back through the dark. He was afraid he might, after all, miss the mark he was aiming for, but at last they landed squarely in front of the dugout.

After carrying the man inside and lowering his bulky, limp body onto the bunk, Fargo scraped the snow plastered on his weather-seamed, haggard face and drew off his outer clothing. His cheeks were white, his fingers were frosted, and when Fargo removed his boots, his left ankle appeared to be swollen. Covering him with a buffalo robe, Fargo worked diligently to restore circulation, estimating he was about forty, five-nine or ten, a hundred-and-fifty or less, and so wiry as to look downright gaunt.

Once the man began to take on some color, Fargo eased up and checked the left ankle. It was bulging, puffy, and discolored, but the skin was unbroken and he couldn't feel any fractured bone. Yet just a bad sprain could be crippling agony out in that storm. No wonder the man had fainted. Now, perversely, as the hoary white faded from his face, a new and ominous shade came into it—not the returning pink of warm flesh but a deep and angry crimson. And he was breathing uneasily, in swift, shallow respirations that ended every few minutes in a wracking cough. Fargo felt his drumbeat pulse, finding his skin clammy hot to the touch.

"Hell, the cold must've got into his lungs. He's burning sick!"

The man's lips twitched. "Cold," he mumbled, his teeth chattering.

Fargo crossed to the stove and lifted a lid. The fire was almost out. Behind the stove were a few sticks that he fed to the firebox, and after looking vainly around for more wood, he turned and saw that the man's eyes were fluttering open. Then, focusing at Fargo, the eyes abruptly snapped wide and stared waxen-bright, a look of fear pinching the man's face.

"You got me, boys," he rasped panting. "I know when I'm done!"

"Relax." Fargo strolled over, calm and pleasant. "Rest easy, friend."

18

"Don't tromp me. Boys, give me a chance to just make a living."

"I'm not any of the boys," Fargo insisted amiably yet firmly. "What's your name? And where's there a woodpile? We got to feed the fire."

Instead of replying, the man began to cough. Something inside him seemed to tear loose and he spat bloody foam, his face flushed from the exertion. His lids, purple and almost transparent, closed over his eyes. A second later he began to mutter, wandering lost again in his own oblivion.

For a moment Fargo looked at the sick man, at the buffalo robe pulsating with rapid breathing due to the lung-searing, brain-boiling fever. But the man wouldn't have needed to hallucinate, Fargo reckoned, to mistake him for an unkempt thug—a big, rough-hewn mountaineer in buckskins. Fargo felt scruffy and knew he looked fierce, his lake-blue eyes bloodshot and red-rimmed from snow glare, his face chapped raw from wind and cold, his tousled black hair and beard untrimmed since leaving Missoula. Perhaps when this guy saw him, it had triggered memories of an old set-to with some hardcases, and his inflamed mind had melted the two events into one.

And that was as much as Fargo cared to speculate, turning his attention to discovering who the man was. Rifling the pockets for some identification, he chanced across cigarette papers, a tobacco pouch, a block of sulfur matches, a pencil stub, a change purse, and a turnip watch engraved with the initials E. C. There were sixty-four dollars in bills and a letter in an envelope folded inside a dog-earned wallet that had E. C. burned in its leather.

The envelope was addressed to Mister Eustace

Chilton, in care of Puckett's Palace, Lewiston, Washington Territory. By the return address, it came from Mrs. G. Clyde Fisher of Sacramento. A brief reading of the letter showed she was Chilton's sister, who'd just given birth to daughter Honoria.

Swiftly and deftly Fargo returned everything as found, grabbed the lantern, and headed for the door. There he paused, glancing back at Eustace Chilton with probing concern. Then, snarling "Damn lung fever!" he stalked outside.

Chilton's paint stood there, patiently waiting. Fargo led it to the stable and stripped it, taking note of the hand-stamped, round-skirted saddle with its carbine scabbard, warbag, and coiled lariat attached. The matching saddlebags were the pair by the pack saddle. He didn't search any of it; right now finding fuel was far more important than probing gear. With the lantern held above his head, he ransacked the stable for something to burn. There wasn't even an armful of slough hay to be had.

Taking his lariat and the one from Chilton's saddle, Fargo tied them together and went back out. With one end attached to himself, and the other end lashed to the front of the stable, he fought his way in a great circle around the latter. He checked every suspicious snow mound that might possibly contain a stack of wood, but the most he came across was a row of corncribs along one side, filled rock-solid with frozen ears of Indian maize. When he repeated his rope trick out around the little dugout, he discovered nothing, period.

Staggering under the mighty drive of the roaring wind, Fargo reeled himself in on the rope and entered the dugout. Inside it was hot, the stove consuming the kindling in a last blaze of glory. He regarded the rough table and chair, wondering how long they would furnish heat, then surveyed the sod walls, the roof. The latter was supported on poles of slender pine, but if he ripped out the poles, the roof would come down. As far as Fargo could tell, there was not one scrap of burnable timber on this stink-finger spread!

Under the buffalo rug on the bunk, Chilton was muttering in a steambath of sweat. The muttering ceased, and Chilton, holding his breath, seemed to listen to something Fargo couldn't hear. Abruptly he groaned and opened wide, igneous eyes, his expression faraway.

"My routes, boys? Take them all," he cried ardently. "I been packing express against weather and grief for two years now, end to mountain end, and you'll take over a prime deal. Ask your boss if my business ain't valuable. Why, for starters I cover the camps at Orofino and Pierce and all those farther east and north." The man paused, laboring for breath.

Fargo tried again: "Listen. We need firewood."

"Sure, it's work. It's my work!" Chilton raged on, gripped by delusion, struggling to rise to his elbow. "Y'all take my Bitterroot route. Cross in my snowshoes with express for them scattered settlers in Hell Gate and Deer Lodge. Me, I'm on my back. You finally rang me in with your men and guns, after I done fought you big cooties single-handed till your tongues was hanging out an—" A paroxysm of coughing seized him and he slipped down sidewise, breathing fast and hawking bloody foam.

"Where's some wood? D'you understand? Wood!"

"No . . . wood," Chilton slurred weakly. "That's

21

what I . . . went after." His lids sagged and he lay back, becoming delerious.

"Shit!" Fargo strode to the table and chair, and began smashing them into pieces that would fit into the stove. The killing wind could blow for three, four days or more. They were out of fuel, Chilton was out of his skull, and he was out of here or out of luck, take his choice. It was sure death to stay. Without a fire, without any warmth, they'd be frozen stiff by morning. If he drifted, gambling his life against the blizzard, he might get through to some line cabin. But it wasn't any gamble with Chilton. Short of a miracle, he'd be dead before the end of the storm.

Fargo had seen his share of miraculous recoveries, but not from grave lung fever or consumption. The few who survived were burnt-out husks. Still, that was not the only fever infecting Eustace Chilton; the fever of express had got into his blood, Fargo sensed, and might be enough of an offsetting tonic to pull him through . . . only to prove fatal for him later, as lethal as lung fever.

Packing express was a big, expanding business. Maybe, when all the route agreements and affiliations were figured in, it would grow to be one of the biggest trades in the West. As always, the big shots fought to get bigger, gobbling or crushing the unprotected and independent small-fry like Eustace Clinton. Things were changing in the express business because it was new and growing, but Fargo had heard the same old story of ruthless arrogance involving railroading, trapping, and ranching.

"Hell, I'll stick here—and try to pull him through," Fargo told himself, gazing across at Clinton's pouchy, fever-scorched face. "Getting soft," he murmured, as he often did. "Getting soft as brown soap."

Soon waves of perishing cold began moving through the dugout, the splintered softwood Fargo was ramming into the stove too light to raise the temperature.

Chilton huddled under the buffalo robe, his teeth rattling and his coughing worsening. "Cold," he whimpered, shivering. "Don't leave me staked out here in the snow, boys. Let me get warm once more an' I'll do just what you say. I'll go away!"

Fargo swore, bitter with frustration and a sense of grim irony. He and Chilton had come safely off the mountains, where incessant storms piled two hundred and fifty inches of snow a year, only to be stranded on the lowlands, where such blizzards were not common. Oh, hereabouts was hardly tropical, he thought sardonically, adding the last chunks of fuel to the fire, but it was livable country for farm-steading wheat or Indian maize or—

Maize?

Struck by a notion, Fargo wheeled and strode to the bunk. "We're going to be hot, Chilton, plenty hot. Hang on," he urged, gripping the sick man's arm. "I just remembered that corn will burn—like coal!"

Chilton ceased whispering, his body grew still, and again he seemed to be listening to some dread voice inaudible to Fargo. Fargo hurriedly left, taking the knotted lariats across to the stable, tying on there as before and heading out for the corncribs. Smashed by the wind, driven time after time to his knees, he plunged onward until, limbs numbed and chest cramped, he reached the row of staked enclosures.

Climbing into the nearest crib, Fargo used his hunting knife to chop loose the ice-locked ears of corn. Staggering under a bulky armload, he returned to the dugout, poked the fire, and after dogged effort got the corn burning. Through the rest of the night Fargo alternately rested, rubbing his chilled flesh, and battled his way out and back from the cribs, fetching corn to feed the horses as well as to heat the dugout, where Eustace Chilton lay torpid, stirring at times, murmuring fitfully.

Toward morning Fargo searched Chilton's saddlebags and pack for anything that might ease the suffering man. Fargo already had checked and found nothing in the dugout, and he soon saw his last chance here was a bust, too. The bags held staples like a currycomb and brush, spare horseshoe, nails, an old Spiller & Burr pistol, extra ammunition, but no surprises. The saddle pack contained the express entrusted to Chilton—some six hundred ounces of freshly washed gold dust and twenty pounds of mail destined for the East via Portland, San Francisco, and the Isthmus of Panama.

Express was founded on trust; it had to be, for deliveries could take six months, sometimes a year. Chilton must have worked hard to gain that trust from suspicious, independent frontier folk, but no question he had it now. Some prospector from back of beyond had given him a buckskin sack heavy with new dust, confident he'd carry it lone-handed over snowbound steeps and ship it out from Lewiston.

Chilton would pick up his incoming express at Lewiston, too. The town was a crossroads and had been a gold-rush gateway since last August, when placer gold had been struck along the Clearwater

River. Soon as the spring thaw hit, Fargo bet, the inflow of gold seekers would swell to a flood, deluging Lewiston on way to the rash of gold camps. Packing their express would fall to trusty Chilton. His one-man, two-nag business would be worth serious money.

Fargo glanced pityingly at the bunk-ridden figure. Chilton would never be worth much again. He was dying. Fargo felt sure he was, lying there prostrate in a feverish stupor, coughing till bloody froth sprang to his lips.

And Fargo could do nothing except stick around on a deathwatch . . .

On the third day the blizzard wind dropped. The sun came out, and Fargo, standing in the doorway, gazed out over low hills that shone like freshly beaten white of egg.

Behind him there was a heap of corn by the stove, and the room was cozily warm. Chilton lay peacefully, shrouded by the buffalo robe, having died in convulsions the prior noon. Fargo had seen no reason to remove the body; he'd no intention to use the bunk or robe, or any desire to go fetch and defrost Chilton later, when the time came to wrap things up.

Well, the time had come, here and now. Closing the door and striding to the stable, Fargo saddled each of the horses and led them into the clear, cold air. The animals resisted feistily, impatient to romp free after three days in the cramped stable. Fargo was just as eager to get out, the stable ripe with profuse horse leavings. But the worst was the corn. Corn can give gas, and, indeed, the horses had gas from feeding solely on corn—so much gas, they had the bloats, their abdomens swollen and aching.

So as well as being rambunctious, the horses were fractious and tetchy. The Ovaro even tried to nip Fargo while being saddled, and wouldn't settle in to being ridden until Fargo had taken it galloping around the clearing a few times in a spirited contest of wills.

The galloping helped work out some gas. The Ovaro passed wind in great blatting thundergusts matched only by the eruptions ripping from the other horses. The gas they had blasted in the stable was thick enough to cut with a knife, a palpable miasma of rancid stench potent enough to have made Fargo's eyes water.

He wrapped Chilton in the robe and trussed him belly-flat across the paint's saddle. He took his rifle and mounted the Ovaro, doubting any ambushers were still lurking about but almost hoping he'd be wrong. Let them try again. Let them get in his way now.

Slowly, under swaying weight, the pack train followed his lead.

Wind slashed down from the foothills, and late in the day there was a brief snow flurry. It was more a nuisance than a threat, and the ride was uneventful apart from sporadic explosions from the horses as they slogged along.

The snow slacked off after dusk. By the time the faltering lights of Lewiston hoved into view, the wind had faded considerably, too.

It was still short of ten o'clock when Fargo rode into the boom camp. Where the Snake and the Clearwater joined, Lewiston had sprawled with reckless vigor. Into it spilled the turbulent traffic from the river heads of Wallula and Umatilla. Lining the main street were a few false-fronts and some frame or log shacks; the rest of the town was canvas, pitched on lanes and open tracts in haphazard arrangements.

While he still had trail ahead of him, Fargo hadn't thought much about strain and worn-out muscles. Now, seeing the yellow lamplight, weariness hit him. Before his rest came the horses, though, and before he tended them, he wanted to tend to the express.

As it happened, the first thing Fargo tended to was Eustace Chilton.

3

Chilton came first by happenstance.

The trail dropped into Lewiston down a barren slope. Too exposed to harbor the living, the weather-swept hill accommodated the dead, a cross-bedded graveyard lodging on a wayside embankment. Spindly pole fencing ran along the front, and by the entrance gate squatted a four-square cabin of faded white clapboard. Lamplight glowed through front window shades, and a squirrel tail of wood smoke plumed from a stovepipe. Suspended from the front porch overhang was a painted wooden sign that read:

L. L. KNAUB • FUNERAL DIRECTOR • MORTICIAN
• MINE EYES HATH SEEN THE GLORY •

Fargo sat on his horse for a moment, deliberating. One man doubling as undertaker and caretaker wasn't uncommon; small rural towns were chronically unable to support either profession, although Fargo suspected that by summer L. L. Knaub would turn enough trade to open a storefront parlor. For now, he roosted a few hundred yards above the Lewiston limits. Fargo wasn't infatuated with the prospect of hiking back up here after partaking of any of the town's warmth, especially with no guarantee that Knaub would still be awake by the time he returned.

Dismounting, Fargo looped reins around fence poles and walked to the front door. Answering his knock was a man of average height, though he looked taller because he was extraordinarily thin. Morose eyes regarded Fargo from a sallow, hatchet-shaped face that lacked a chin but had wattles for a neck. Evidently Fargo had interrupted him in shirt-sleeves, for he was buttoning a black cutaway frock coat, in a deliberate way that only added to his melancholy mien.

"Good evening," he said from down deep around his boots. "Launcelot Lorenzo Knaub, mortician, at your service."

"Not mine, thanks," Fargo said, and took Knaub out to the paint. Then they took Chilton into the cabin, threading past stacks of cheap coffins of raw pine, and past one displayed on sawhorses, a more expensive casket painted gold and sporting bronzed iron handles. The two men were cautious and slow, the robe-wrapped deadweight swinging laxly between them, and finally made it across the front and into the rear room.

Once inside, Knaub dropped the legs and said, "Hold him steady."

Fargo propped Chilton against the wall. Knaub lit a lantern, closed the door, then picked up the legs again, and they slid Chilton onto a metal-clad table. Nearby was a smaller table arrayed with instruments, towels, and a washbasin, where Knaub spent some minutes scrubbing his hands, conversing in doleful tones. But Fargo was deaf, absorbed in thought. Questions were still unresolved despite his ruminating these past days, and those involving Chilton had to be brought to terms very rapidly.

Drying his hands, Knaub opened the robe—and gasped. "Chilton!"

"No, it's not," Fargo countered.

"It certainly is! Why, I'd know Eustace Chilton anywhere," Knaub argued indignantly. "Maybe there isn't no law here yet, but I won't be party to—"

"Don't think it's so easy recognizing Chilton. Just as this last storm broke, I was mistaken for him. I'd one packhorse, a dun of near color and build to his chestnut packer, which's maybe why it got shot. I got shot at, too," Fargo added, his bearded lips flattening in a wry grin. "No, our buddy here didn't die of lead poisoning. He died naturally, of lung fever."

Knaub frowned. "A bullet would've been more merciful. Aye, and I know for a fact Eustace made no provisions," he groused mournfully, gingerly peeling back some clothing. "Goes to show you, arranging beforehand sure helps to satisfy everyone concerned. Now he'll have to be laid out without a lining to protect him from the splinters or a—"

"Here, contact his sister for arrangements," Fargo cut in, handing Knaub the letter from Mrs. G. Clyde Fisher. The lantern shed a vapid glow that seemed to accentuate the gloom, and there was a pungent odor, a cloying mix of embalming fluids and rosewater that gave Fargo the willies as he withdrew fifty dollars of his own money and stuffed the bills in Knaub's breast pocket.

Knaub brightened considerably. "Sage man, sir, and most generous. For this, Eustace shall embark on his final eternal journey in comfort and style, including satin lining, pallbearers, and a guaranteed four mourners."

"No. No service, none. I don't want anyone to hear of his death."

"But—but I don't understand. Surely you can't keep his death a secret forever. And what of his sister, Mrs. Fisher?"

"She won't come here. Ship the body to her or bury it here, whichever she wishes. Put him in a bone box for now, and nail the lid down tight. He'll keep outside," Fargo directed, his lean grin fading as he eyed the appalled mortician. "If anybody gets curious, tell 'em he's Mr. G. Clyde Fisher. The ruse won't be for long. I can't say how long, but you'll know when it's done."

"Take back your money. I refuse, I won't be party to—"

"I know. What I don't know is if you're a friend of Chilton's."

"Why, yes, I suppose. Much as all his travelin' would allow."

"Alright, then, listen up. Whoever mistook me for Chilton, I reckon, has been hounding him something fierce. Now, I've got his stuff, most of which I'll leave here or at the livery stable, but I'll hand in the express and see if I can't parley it into some personal satisfaction. Point is, if Chilton is dead, the men who wanted him dead will sink out of sight. They'll escape."

"Yes, I see . . . Eustace Chilton isn't dead until we make him dead." Knaub nodded, stroking his wattles. Then with a disparaging cluck, he walked around Fargo with a measuring eye. "No question.

Standard size will squeeze you. Will pine suffice or do you prefer select hardwoods?"

Fargo swiveled with him, feeling the hairs on the back of his neck begin to prickle. "Hold on. Is your business so bad that you've got to find customers while they're still kicking?"

Knaub shook his head, sighing. "I'm working more than is comfortable now, truth to tell, since the gold strike. We've had a pack of trail wolves running loose lately. They've a way of knowing where a man is bound, and they'll jump him when the odds are all in their favor." Knaub added somewhat reprovingly, "You go out alone, flimflamming yarns about poor Eustace, and for you, a week may be stretching it."

"Fatal as all that, eh? Well, let me ponder it some."

The mortician looked distinctly morose now. "I wouldn't tarry overly long, sir. Eustace, he didn't go prepared, and arrangements should be made by choice rather than chance."

"I'm not quite prepared, either," Fargo said, and after shaking hands, he headed for the door. As he started into the front room, he called back, "I'm still young yet."

"The dumb die young," Knaub sighed reverently.

Closing the front door behind him, Fargo untethered the horses, swung asaddle, and led the way on down the slope into the town proper—or improper, as the case may be. Snow in the walkless street had been churned to a muddy paste under the clutter of restless men, horses, and wagons that still filled the roadway. Fargo let his train pick its slow passage through.

He reined in before one of the log buildings, on the facade of which was crudely painted the name, PUCKETT'S PALACE. Hiram Puckett had operated a trading post here before gold was dreamed of, Fargo knew, and the last time Fargo had come through, Puckett had just initiated an express run from Lewiston by way of The Dalles to Portland, tying in there with Wells, Fargo & Company.

Hitching his horses to the rack in front of the trading post, Fargo tossed a warning to those nearby: "Don't get too close to 'em. They're feeling cross-grained today, and're liable to bite a hunk out of you."

He unstrapped the express pack and heaved it over one shoulder, kneeing open the door. The blast from a roaring stove hit him at once, making his cheeks burn as if hot iron had been pressed against them. The main room was big, with a counter and shelves along one side and a whipsawed-plank bar along the other. In between were the inevitable gambling tables, most of them active but not crowded with players.

Fargo pushed along between the tables. The air was blurred with cigar and lamp-oil smoke, and the smells of whiskey and beer made his throat dry. Catching a glimpse of Hi Puckett behind the counter, at the back where twin-panned scales had been built in front of the post's armoire-sized stand-up safe, Fargo headed toward the proprietor, studying the man's features. Puckett had no reason to recall the Trailsman and Fargo would have been surprised if he had, yet Fargo knew him by sight and reputation. A man of wide girth and unflagging joviality, Puckett was generally well thought of, an asset to the gold camps with his dust bank. Here a man could store his poke, have a letter written, a message relayed, even get a bottle on credit maybe, or a generous grubstake. As could be expected under the circumstances, Puckett carried the friendly moniker of Hi Pockets.

An extra lamp had been hung from the rafters above the big balances, and its hazy yellow light glinted on the slivers of shiny scalp showing through Puckett's thinning black hair. At the moment he was weighing out a dust poke, exacting his storage fee, and taking up the receipt. A red-shirted miner stood across the unpainted pine counter, watching with acquiescence while Puckett thimbled some dust into the house poke. It was, by all appearances, an honest transaction, with no objection anywhere.

The deal concluded, the miner tramped the length of the room, steering clear of the bar and trying to look casual, for a man didn't advertise his movements or his fortune more than he could help with human vultures preying on the trails. But according to the mortician, Fargo remembered, the crooks seemed to have a way of knowing such things. Without being able to pin down exactly why, he couldn't help thinking that when a man figured he'd made his stake and decided to pull out, good ol' Hi Pockets would be the one to always know it.

Reaching the counter, Fargo set the pack down and grinned confidently. Puckett had a cigar in his right hand, which jerked slightly as he brought his eyes to bear with a startled look. He was about to say something—probably about recognizing Chilton's pack, Fargo sensed—when someone burst out with a raucous laugh, followed by a surging and shifting at the bar that drew their attention.

A young man in a miner's outfit, complete to laced boots and stiff-brimmed Stetson, had risen from a poker table and now was yelling at the bartender. "Pour a round for all them idiot card-sharps there," he crowed, his voice slurring as if he'd imbibed a drink too many. "It's on me, but hell, they been paying for it!"

Puckett gave a grunt. "Joel Dumas. Turned up some pretty good color a few weeks ago, and he's been on a howl ever since. He likes to hooraw when he wins good. Can't fault him. His wins are few and far between. Now then, stranger, what's your business with this-here pack?"

"Chilton's business," Fargo replied heartily. "Fargo's the name, Skye Fargo. Eustace needed me to help bring in his express and, well, here it is. Lots of mail and six hundred ounces, maybe a little more. Best load Eustace has collected so far, and the start of bigger things yet."

Puckett kept his hands where they were on the counter. "Things are already big, Mr. Fargo, too big," he said thoughtfully. "I'm afraid I can't handle Chilton's stuff any longer."

"What do you mean, can't handle it? You've got an agreement with Eustace, don't you?"

"We never put one on a contract basis," Puckett countered. "I was going to tell him when he came in this time, but since you did in his stead, I guess you'll just have to pass along to him that it's over. He's made some money; he'll have to let it go at that. The simple fact is that this express thing has grown too large for him to swing, with or without your help, no hard feelings. It's going to take money and backing. They've got strikes up by Excelsior, y'know, and there're whiffs all across the Bitterroots."

"That's why Eustace is hereabouts. That's what he's been going after."

Puckett turned the cigar in his fingers. "Chilton can't go after it. He's got no way to move his express west."

"Your idea," Fargo asked evenly, "is to choke him off?"

"Not precisely. I'm trying to save him trouble, is all."

"Chilton has taken care of his own trouble till now."

"Not this much of it."

"Yeah?" Fargo leaned forward, anger sharpening his blue eyes. "Who's in on this with you, Hi Pockets?"

"Why, you got me wrong, I—"

"Who?"

"N—Nehalem, Giles Nehalem. He's new here, in from California."

"And where do I find him?"

"I dunno, but he often stops by 'twixt eleven and midnight."

"Okay. Safekeep Eustace's pack in the meanwhile."

"Now, look, I just finished telling you, you—"

"Stow it. You never know what me and Nehalem might work out." Melted snow from Fargo's hat was running from its brim, and he brushed the hat off to keep his hands busy, away from Puckett's face. Be companionable, he told himself. He watched Puckett stare at his heavy-knuckled fingers kneading the hat brim. The trader then took the pack off the counter and shoved it inside the tall safe. Fargo thanked him in a clipped voice, adding, "The livery stable looked closed-up dark when I rode by. Where's the hostler bed down?"

"At the stable. But he ain't turned in yet." Puckett gestured toward the poker table where Joel Dumas was playing cards. "He's sitting over there. The ol' heller's name is Modoc Thorne."

"I'll be back." Fargo turned and thrust through the crowd.

4

Skye Fargo had no trouble picking out the hostler, Modoc Thorne, from the four players seated at the table.

Besides Dumas, there were two husky laborers, the larger and more muscular of them having sooty grime under his fingernails and in the pores of his jowly face, indicating he was a blacksmith by trade. The fourth man had enormous shoulders and long arms, a square-lined face dominated by a brushy gray moustache, and fathomless eyes under beetling gray brows. Clad in range garb, he wore a .44 Remington high on the left side, cross-draw fashion, butt forward. And he exuded the unmistakable odors of musty hay and sweaty leather.

Fargo waited while they played out the hand, which the fourth man won with queens up. Then he asked him, "Modoc Thorne?" The man nodded as he raked in the pot, and Fargo went on to tell him he had four horses needing care and feed.

"Unless they're footsore frazzled," Thorne replied, gravel-voiced, "I'd plumb appreciate staying for a few more hands. You're welcome to sit in."

Though his natural inclination was to tend the horses, Fargo saw no great harm in a short delay. Moreover, he was far from finished with Hi Pockets and the unknown Giles Nehalem, and might well pick up some useful information here or from Thorne—a hostler, after all, was also in a position to know of local goings-on, as well as of any horses with toed-in forehoofs.

"Don't mind if I do," Fargo allowed affably, removing his coat and taking the vacant chair between Joel Dumas and the blacksmith. As the deal passed around the table, he looked for signs of cheating, but the game appeared honest, no ringers or marked cards, nothing wilder than straight draw or stud. The play was desultory, pots generally low and going back and forth, although Dumas was stewed and mostly lost.

When Dumas lost on two pairs against Fargo's three tens, he flung his cards down and glowered at Fargo. "Dammit, you dealt that round."

"It was my turn," Fargo replied curtly, gathering in the deck. He had shuffled and dealt methodically, carefully, to avoid any hint of cardsharping; with a little luck he had bluffed the stronger hands into folding. And now he was in no mood to take guff off a chump who'd stayed on two small pair.

The blacksmith leaned across, facing Dumas. "If the game's too stiff, kid, why don't you drop out."

"Why don't you, Vern Koehler! Drop out, my ass!"

"Then here, it's your turn," Fargo growled, pushing the deck toward Dumas. "Now, shut up your bleating and deal. This isn't penny ante."

The game resumed. Dumas slouched in his chair, drinking, wagering increasingly reckless and imprudent sums. His lanky tanned features were marred by a petulantly sneering mouth, and by eyes booze-burnished with the dream of winning and the dread of losing. His chips continued dwindling rapidly under the relaxed yet seasoned playing of the others.

When the deal reached Fargo again, he declared, "Straight draw. Modoc, what say we go take care of my horses after this round."

Modoc agreed, and immediately raised after Dumas opened. The betting went around twice, run up by Dumas and Modoc, then Fargo dealt the draw cards. The laborer gave one look and withdrew from play. Modoc clutched his cards close, smirking slyly as if he had a secret strength. Dumas wet his lips and fidgeted with his cards, obviously excited by the power of his hand. The blacksmith, as usual, glared around as though silently daring them to beat him. Fargo took three cards and, pleased by the draw, laid his hand facedown on the table and said to Dumas, "Up to you."

Dumas threw in two chips. That wouldn't drive out any player, Fargo knew; Dumas hoped they'd stay in, fatten the pot, evidently convinced they couldn't win and he wouldn't lose.

So, apparently, was Modoc Thorne. "I'll raise it by five bucks."

In a small stakes game, five dollars was a decisive bet. The blacksmith tossed in his hand, cussing and shaking his head. Fargo, though, was willing to gamble Thorne was bluffing. "Covered, plus ten more."

"Makes it fifteen to me, eh?" Dumas grinned scornfully at Fargo and then Thorne. "Well, I'll double the jack and make it twenty-five to you, Modoc."

Thorne stroked his moustache and then laughed abruptly. "Hell, my hand ain't worth twenty-five cents." He folded, dropping out like he'd wanted others to do; he had, after all, been bluffing.

"So back to you." Dumas grinned snidely at Fargo. "Well? Chuck in your cards or fifteen bucks."

Fargo doubted Dumas was bluffing—or could bluff, for that matter. The man had all the sly subtlety of a buffalo prick. Having read this in Dumas from the start, Fargo had never pinned hopes on him bluffing, but gambled on him bungling. Careless, witless, blindly taking too much for granted, Dumas could louse up at any time in any damnfool way, and Fargo suspected Dumas already had, by overestimating the strength of his hand. And betting that Dumas's hand was not good enough to beat his own, Fargo chucked the fifteen dollars and another ten into the pot.

Dumas eyed Fargo smugly. "Willing to take the limit off?"

"Up to you," Fargo murmured nonchalantly.

Thorne said hastily, "Maybe you best think twice, Joel."

"Mind your own damn affairs," Dumas snapped. "I'll raise you fifty dollars, Fargo, for starters."

His expression unchanged, Fargo watched Dumas count chips into the heap in the center of the table. When Dumas was done, Fargo bought chips from an adjoining poker table, gave Thorne some bills to go buy more from Hi Pockets, then pushed two measured stacks forward. "You're in a man's game now," he told Dumas. "Your fifty and a hundred on top of it."

"And a hundred more," Dumas said sharply—and a mite too quickly, for he ran out of chips and added what money he carried, and still came up fifty-six dollars short.

Fargo sat back silent, expressionless, watching Dumas sweat. Dumas kept pawing through his pockets and glancing around nervously, as if praying for a miracle, but it was what he *didn't* do that intrigued Fargo more. For one, he looked pleadingly at the others but didn't ask any of them for money, and they didn't offer. Dumas didn't go to Hi Pockets and mooch a short-term loan, either, though Hi Pockets might have a policy against loaning on poker hands. Still, it was odd Dumas didn't at least try. Nor did he say he'd go get some of his gold, but he could well have blown his strike by now and be flat broke.

Not quite. "How much will you give me for this?" Dumas asked huskily. He held up a diamond ring, while his hungry eyes darted from player to player.

Fargo said, "Better keep it for a stake, just in case you lose."

"Never mind about that," Dumas snapped. "Are you afraid I'll stage a comeback?"

"Hardly." Fargo gave a low, caustic chuckle. He picked up the ring, regarded it closely, held it to the light, and remarked, "This's a lady's ring."

"Well, what about it?"

"About a hundred," Fargo replied, pushing a stack of chips toward Dumas. He put the ring in his pants pocket, then moved his money in to cover Dumas's raise and said quietly, "I'll bump it, 'less you want to call it now."

"Right now will do," Dumas said, admiring the mountainous pot.

Fargo laid his hand out without preamble—three aces and two sixes. "Aces full. Top that if you can."

Dumas looked at his cards and gnawed his lip. After a moment he looked up hotly and slammed his cards on the table. They fell face up and scattered a little way apart—a king-high flush of diamonds.

The blacksmith said, "Full house beats a flush, kid. You shouldn't show the losing hand."

Dumas ignored him, standing up and staring at Fargo. "You sure deal yourself lucky hands, don't you think?" he said tightly.

"That's right," Fargo replied calmly. He made no move to scoop in his winnings but sat watching Dumas cautiously. "Pure lady luck."

Thorne, shoving his chair back, said harshly, "Drop it, Joel."

"Hell I will!" Dumas retorted. "Fargo knew all along what I had in my hand. You see how all-fired willing he was to kill the limit?"

The laborer shouted, "He did it to oblige you, kid!"

"Now shut up before you end up good and dead!" Thorne yelled.

"Damn you all, damn you!" Dumas swore loudly, "A perfect stranger horns in on our game, cheats us blue, and you just let him get away with it! You—"

"Easy there!" someone warned.

But Dumas flung off a restraining arm and shook his knotted fists at Fargo. "You—you're a crooked tinhorn hiding in grubbies!" he raged, half-sobbing, and with a sudden, frantic effort, he dived for the revolver at his hip.

Fargo had not moved up to that moment. Now, without the appearance of hurry and yet with no wasted motions, he kicked his chair back and leaped to face Dumas. He could have killed Dumas then and there; a great many men would have, and there was every excuse in the world for it. Instead Fargo sprang at Dumas, catching his hand on the draw, and the shot went wild through the ceiling.

"Drop the gun," he snarled.

"Damn you, you—"

"Drop it, or I'll break your arm."

Dumas writhed and squirmed, trying to tear himself loose. His revolver went off again and a shot smashed one of the lamps hanging from the ceiling. Fargo rushed him against the nearest wall, bent his arm behind his back, and twisted his wrist in a hold that made the young man cry out with pain. He dropped the gun and started to slump.

Fargo gathered Dumas's collar in his fist and hauled him straight up again on his feet. He yanked Dumas forward until his face was only a foot away, put a piratical glint in his eye, and spoke in a wicked half-whisper: "You're overdue for a lesson, sonny. Modoc Thorne was dead right. I've shot men in their bathtubs and outhouses for less than you've jawed tonight. Any more of your sass, I'll cut your tongue out at the roots, and then I'll shoot you in both kneecaps and toss you in the Snake. Understand?"

Joel Dumas's mouth was working. Fargo shoved him tumbling across the room, arms windmilling. He sprawled over the faro table, crashed down on the floor with a couple of chairs on top of him.

Then the front door banged open and a woman stood on the threshold, glancing inquisitively about the smoke-filled room. Her gaze settled on Dumas as he rose on wobbly legs, his face bruised and bleeding. With a little cry she ran to him and put her arms about him, aiding him to his feet.

She somehow threw a spell over the rough-clad, rough-mannered men. The din died, and the men edged away and backward. She was a young woman, in her early twenties, very pretty in her tan mackinaw and moosehide moccasins. Her toque was many-hued, and that part of her hair beneath it shimmered like spun gold. Her eyes were two dark pools of anger and indignation as she looked over the men.

"Who did this?" she cried.

The men scuffled about uneasily. A bartender breathed into a glass and polished it with a great show of industry while his boss, Hi Pockets, gazed at the ceiling and whistled noiselessly. The laborer cleared his throat and ventured:

"Miss, he brung it on hisself, he did. We was playing cards and he lost right along, and when he was cleaned out he called a man crooked."

"Well, I shouldn't be surprised if you were crooked," she retorted hotly. "You look like a crooked man, anyhow. You are all wolves, all of you! Look at his poor face. You—you must have kicked him when he was down!"

"Miss, it wasn't me—"

"I'm the man, miss," Fargo cut in, coming forward.

"Then you—you kicked him, you brute!"

"No. I beat him at cards," Fargo countered evenly. "I cleaned him out and he accused me of cheating. He pulled his gun and I took it away from him and flung him off. He fell over a table and some chairs, is all."

"You're just an oily-tongued gambler," she told Fargo. "I know your type, waiting and sitting in the warm dives and bilking the men who hunt for gold. You haven't the courage to tackle the wilderness trails. It takes a man to do that."

She dragged Dumas toward the door. A man opened it and the two disappeared.

In the room the tension relaxed. Men began to move about. Glasses clinked at the bar. The blacksmith regarded the laborer, saying, "You got more balls than me, Howard. I ain't afeared of nothing that walks, crawls, hops, or flies, nothing 'cept gals on tirades and guys who're strike drunk."

The laborer laughed. Modoc Thorne said, "The kid's probably all right. I seen older men than he is go crazy thataway. Just needs sense pounded into him."

"He'll get it," Fargo said, scooping in the pot, "if somebody doesn't kill him first."

"I reckon that's what's got his sister scared upset. Amity Dumas came up from Portland last week, and she's sure had her hands full, looking after Joel," Thorne commented. "Okay, let me grab my coat and buy a bottle, and we'll get to your horses."

Fargo nodded and went to cash in his chips. Thorne got delayed at the bar, trying to buy his bottle, so Fargo motioned to meet him outside, and headed for the door. He was just stepping out when he heard his Ovaro's distinctive whinny and a man's harsh voice:

"Hold the devil, Trent, while I—" The voice choked off.

Fargo launched from the doorway, catching a swift look at the setup. Ugly and stout, with a shaved, malformed head, a man was scrambling under the rack, trying to dodge the rearing Ovaro, his face ashen, his hat lying in the snow. Another man, taller and heavier and with a fat tomato of a nose, was attempting to grab the horse's bit without being bitten in turn.

The bald man didn't see Fargo sprinting toward him. He was palming a revolver, murder in his eyes. "I'll l'arn that nag to fart in my face."

Fargo reached out and yanked him off balance. The man gave a wild yelp and tried to bring his revolver up. Fargo knocked it out of his hand and rammed his fist into the man's started chops. The man caromed against the cross pole of the rack so hard that he splintered it. He dropped, momentarily stunned and breathless.

The man trying to grab the reins jerked for his pistol. He only drew partway as Fargo, springing the short distance, caught him in the belly with a straight-arm knuckler. The man careened back, slamming the front walls of the trading post, his pistol flying, then dropped like a sack of potatoes.

The bald man was dragging himself away, turning a stricken face to the Ovaro, which was rearing over him. Fargo's soothing voice calmed his horse until it merely pawed and snorted testily. The second man, gasping for air, stumbled forward with one hand clutching his belly and his other fumbling for his pistol.

Fargo kicked the pistol aside. "Next time you want to fool around with any horse, make sure you get permission."

The second man, the one named Trent, grimaced and wheezed, "Hell, Damrow only wanted a look at him."

"Damrow must be nearsighted."

Damrow was rising to his feet, and he rose swinging. He'd crawled feebly until he was almost behind Fargo, acting as though the fight was out of him, and then lashed out to catch Fargo unaware. He nearly succeeded, but for Fargo glimpsing his move at the last instant.

A roundhousing haymaker crunched Fargo's jaw before he could fully swerve aside. The blow's meaty impact sent him staggering. Wincing with pain, Fargo shook his head to clear it, falling back to regain his footing, his left heel accidently stomping Trent's wrist, Trent having used Damrow's sneak attack to try again for his pistol. Trent reeled, and along with the howls Fargo could also hear sounds of men gathering, coming mostly from the trading post. The noises were confused, his head was still ringing, but Fargo didn't pay them any attention anyway, dismissing all vagrant subjects from his consciousness to focus on Damrow.

"Stand clear, boys, give him room to fall," Damrow called, contemptuous with confidence. "He's big and'll hit hard."

"He ain't fallin', Damrow," Fargo heard one of the bystanders say.

"He's gonna hit dirt," Damrow growled savagely. "Any of you gents know I only has to tap once to snuff an hombre's lights out."

It was then Fargo struck back with a jolting uppercut, followed by a one-two combination. His right punch started from his shoulder, went slightly upward, then smashed down like a club. Damrow tried to jerk his head backward to save himself, and he did, perhaps, save himself a broken skull. As it was, Fargo's fist slashed down across his forehead, nose, and chin, instantly turning his face into a blob of red and driving Damrow almost to his knees. While he was in that squatting position, Fargo's left fist hammered into his chest and hurled him, squawling, back into the circle of onlookers, where he lay still.

Fargo turned slightly as Trent dived at him with a yell. A backward swing of Fargo's arm caught Trent in the throat, flipping him around. Fargo's hand speared out and took him by the neck while his other hand snared the slack in his pants. Lifting him, Fargo gave him a twirl and sent him sailing through the doorway just as a bartender with a table-leg truncheon was about to step out. The man's body hit the bartender solidly and sent him tumbling back inside with a grunt of gasping breath. The door swung shut, masking from view the scene of the resounding crash.

"Gawd, he downed Damrow right smart. An' Trent, he's still seeing stars," Fargo heard somebody declare in awe.

Another gawker guffawed. "He tuckered the cream o' Hi Pockets' bouncers."

Without comment Fargo brushed himself off and moved toward his Ovaro and the other horses. Behind him the trading-post door opened, and out of the corner of his eye he saw Modoc Thorne step outside. Fargo stiffened, every muscle in his body taut.

Modoc Thorne had on his coat, and the coat was made of canvas.

5

A fury of blood surged to Skye Fargo's temples.

Be companionable, he reminded himself. One canvas storm coat proved nothing. Still, it was something to go on. Anger and alert suspicion tugged at his weariness, yet there was no sign of enmity on his face, except for the fact that one eye was squinting and his lips were drawn partly back from clenched teeth as he watched Modoc Thorne come from the trading-post doorway.

"Wish I'd seen the first of it, but let's scat before some of Hi Pockets' buckos make more of it," Thorne suggested with a friendly smile. "Get the rest of your string. I'll take your pinto."

"Don't try," Fargo cautioned. "It's acting meaner than sin today."

"I've always had a way with wild critters. Tamed a bear once, and had no end of moose eatin' out of my hand. I even gentled a cougar—a young'un, but plenty savage just the same."

As he spoke, Thorne was approaching Fargo's horse. Foul-tempered from gas and nervously agitated by the uproar, the Ovaro laid its ears back, wrenching its hitchrail-tied reins and kicking skittishly. Thorne eased closer, gentle in his motions, confident in manner. The horse reared to strike out with its forehoofs, white-eyed, snorting through clenched teeth at one end and rumbling flatulently out the other.

"Back off, you'll get hurt," Fargo warned.

Thorne didn't answer. Holding his breath, he reached out as the Ovaro shook its head, and rubbed the animal's nose. A shudder ran through the mount, and it put its ears forward and nickered softly.

"Well, I'll be damned," Fargo exclaimed.

"You should be, for feeding your cayuse skunk cabbage," Thorne gasped, holding his nose. Then, as Fargo fell in with the other three horses and they began heading up the street to the livery, Thorne observed, "That paint and chestnut mare of yours either got twin-foals, or I last seen 'em with Eustace Chilton."

"They're his. I'm leaving them off with you."

The mare backfired. Thorne swore. "When's Chilton picking 'em up?"

"He didn't say," Fargo hedged. "Does my pack-horse look familiar, too?"

Eying the dapple mare, Thorne shook his head. "Carry a brand?"

"The Lazy-A, and was ridden by a red-bearded man."

"No Lazy-A hereabouts. I don't much remember people, never could."

"How about a horse whose off front hoof toes in?"

"That I'd recall, but nope, sorry. I'm not a vet or smithy, and there're one or two broncs around I happen not to stable," Thorne added facetiously.

Fargo let it drop, a sudden breezy gust chilling him, almost tearing off his hat. He scrunched his hat down tighter and raised his broad collar to shield himself from the cold, the night frigid enough to stiffen gloved fingers and make leading the horses a difficult task.

Reaching the livery, they walked the horses into the dark barn and closed the double-door entrance. Cupping their hands, having trouble thumb-striking Swedish matches aflame against the swirling drafts, they located lanterns and were about to light them when the horses loosened a blistering salvo. Matches guttering, they were plunged into darkness as Thorne shouted, "Don't light nothing! The fumes might explode!" After a choking moment he wheezed, "On second thought, strike up and let's hope they do."

The wind outside blew in sporadic rushes, rapidly frittering and dying to calm lulls. Blustering currents whipped through the slapdash-built barn, dissipating the vapors and freshening the air, while the galvanized-sheet roof flapped like an angry bird, making the lamps flicker violently as Fargo helped Thorne provide the horses rubdowns, feed, and stalls.

Thorne conversed idly, usually about weather or horses. Fargo responded occasionally, innocuous and impersonal, avoiding discussions that could draw him out. As in poker, the less he revealed, the less his opponents could outmaneuver him; the more he learned of them, the more he could anticipate their moves. Beyond that, poker and life in general seemed to be won on luck and by playing the percentages.

When the bulk of work was done, and the horses were drowsily munching oats in their stalls, Fargo left Thorne to finish up and went to get his warbag.

Thorne asked, "Going to Hi Pockets'?"

Fargo gave him a startled frown. "Why?"

"I'm going again." Thorne gestured toward the

shedlike supply room near the back, half filled with bagged feed grain. "Not much, but it's a right dry place. And with this bottle dry, I'm feelin' a need that Pockets' can satisfy. You coming, too? I'd cotton the company."

"I might drop in later, after I see about food and a room."

"Buckhorn Hotel, down past Pockets'," Thorne directed. "The dining room closes about twelve-thirty. Passable food, more or less, depending on your constitution, but I haven't heard of any not passing eventually. Say, before you go, tell me how in our poker game you always knew when I was bluffing. I know I did something that tipped my hand, but I'm stumped what it might be."

"Simple." Grinning, Fargo slung his warbag across his shoulders. "You wiggled your ears," he said, and headed for the entrance.

"Dammit! I'll sure think twice before betting you again!" Thorne yelled after him, then choked, sputtered, and burst into guffaws.

Fargo headed across the livery yard, the spasmodic breeze he had felt earlier now whuffing along, swirling powdery wafts of snow in eddies before it. Mulling over Modoc Thorne, he came away feeling the man was experienced around animals and a competent hostler. Thorne was no phony, or a stoved-up drunkard like so many hostlers were. True, he was a hard drinker—he had, with Fargo, polished off that bottle of his—yet he showed no signs of alcoholism, nor had he taken a drink during the card game. All his talk about a dry bottle was sheer crap, which only made him sound like some souse needing to tuck a bottle to bed with him at night.

That image, Fargo reckoned as he turned down

the street, did not fit Modoc Thorne. It fit stewbum hostlers, though. So in that sense, Thorne's stewbum talk fit his role as hostler. Thorne himself was a liar, not a lush.

Whatever else Thorne was, as a hostler he was a common man of the common herd, with more trail smarts than book learning, and just enough hint of country bumpkin to add a regional flavor. Even his revolver looked clumsy, thrust higher than the normal shell-belted thigh holster or the casual sticking of a pistol into one's trousers. But again Thorne's looks were deceiving. Fargo bet more than one slick dude had been fooled into overconfidence. Up close, in the barn, he had seen that the older, well-used Remington was in prime condition, reflecting assiduous care. It convinced Fargo that Modoc Thorne knew what he was doing, which meant that somewhere over the years, Thorne had mastered the difficult yet extremely fast cross-draw.

Not exactly an average talent of an average hostler.

There was more to this man in the canvas coat than met the eye.

The sky was stinging cold and there was little activity on the street, even in front of Pocket's noisy trading post. A short way past the post, Fargo could make out the two-storied, log-walled Buckhorn Hotel across the street, and headed diagonally toward it, boots crunching through the thin icing of snow on the street. Reaching the front porch of the hotel, he had opened the door and started inside when a passing gust tore the door from his grip and slammed it behind him as he stepped into the lobby.

New to Fargo, the Buckhorn Hotel had been recently built. The bare timber paneling the walls was unpainted, and there was a carpet with a flowing rose pattern on the floor. Through scarlet portieres on his left was the dining room: square, lacking a counter, a smattering of customers at four stubby tables with their benches lined perpendicular to the archway. As he approached the registration desk near the banistered staircase, a big lumpy woman arose from an overstuffed armchair next to the pigeonholed backboard and squinted at him.

"Room Twen'-two, second floor," she grumbled drowsily, plunking a key down after Fargo had signed the register and paid for the night. "No drinkin', no sportin', no roughhousin', and never no refunds."

"No doubt," Fargo murmured, and, hefting his warbag, went upstairs to his room. It was simple, utilitarian, with the standard bed on which he dumped his bag, a mirrored bureau with a pitcher, basin, and an oil lamp that he lit, and a single window whose shade he pulled. Cleaning up a bit, he stowed his gear and went back downstairs to the dining room, where he took an empty table near the back.

A paunchy man in a bib apron and dungarees came out from the kitchen, scratching his hairy chest through the sides of his apron. "Steak, 'tatoes, and coffee," he said belligerently. "Okay by you?"

"Suppose so," Fargo replied, seeing no point in arguing.

The food turned out to be inedible, and Fargo was wresting the gristly slab of meat on his plate when Amity Dumas entered. Spotting him, she crossed to his table and sat down across from him, looking somewhat embarrassed.

"Mr. Fargo, I'm Joel Dumas's sister, and naturally I was upset by him losing all his money at cards," she began hurriedly. "But I heard later that it was Joel's fault and that you merely took his gun away from him. I ought to apologize."

"No need. Best thing you can do is help him find some sense before it's too late for him."

Amity's eyes focused on him. After a moment's silence she said, "You could have killed him. Thank you for not killing him."

"Your thanks aren't needed, either. I didn't do it to oblige you."

"Why did you?"

Fargo shrugged. "Maybe I'm tired of seeing guys die over nothing."

He was watching Amity Dumas and her eyes were direct against his. But in a moment she shook herself from their locked glance and looked down, opening her bag. "This will seem strange to you, Mr. Fargo, but I'm led to believe I can trust you. I want you to keep something for me. For two hours. Then bring it to Room Nine, here in the hotel. I can't explain it until then."

Before Fargo could answer, she had lifted something out of her bag, screened by the table, and he felt something heavy drop into his lap. The girl rose without looking at him again and hastened out of the dining room.

It was a dust poke. Fargo dropped it into his coat pocket quickly, surprised and puzzled. From its heft, there would be a couple of thousand dollars in it. Calling "Wait!" he started after Amity, only to be blocked by the chef with his hand drawn, demanding payment.

"Leftovers," the chef complained, frowning as Fargo paid him. "Don't like my cooking?"

"Adore it," Fargo replied testily, frustrated, knowing he was too late and the girl had gone. Struck by a suspicious hunch, he then asked the chef, "Can you wrap up my leftovers, so I can take 'em along in case I get hungry later?"

"I guess." The chef carried the plate into the kitchen, and after a moment, returned with the uneaten steak wrapped and string-tied in brown butcher paper. "I gets the same gnawings at night myself," he confided.

Thanking him, Fargo went out to the lobby desk, wanting to examine the register to find out who was listed for Room Nine. The fat woman was asleep, head resting on her chins, but as he leaned over the counter she awakened and cast him a sullen eye. Fargo smiled. "You got a safe here?"

The woman nodded. "There's an extra charge for using it."

"Figures," Fargo muttered, and went up to his room. Inside, door locked, he flung the meat out the window and wrapped Amity's gold-dust poke in the paper. Then taking the string-tied parcel downstairs, he placed it on the desk and told the woman, "Hold on to this for a couple of hours, and never mind what's in it."

"Couldn't care less, Mister. The rats might, by the greasy smell of it. That'll be three bucks."

Paying, Fargo asked politely, "Miss Dumas's room?"

"Nine, down the hall."

He started toward the ground floor corridor.

"She ain't in," the woman said.

"Thanks," Fargo answered, and kept walking.

"Miss Dumas ain't in," the woman snapped louder, "and that means visitors for Miss Dumas ain't going to go see her."

Fargo glanced speculatively along the dim hallway, but he did not go on; he turned and went out of the hotel. He was tired but now was held up for at least two hours, whether or not Giles Nehalem showed at Hi Pockets' place. It piqued him to wonder why Amity Dumas hadn't turned her poke over to Hi Pockets the way everyone else did. Why entrust it to a stranger, even if he was thought to be honest . . . unless he was reckoned to be gullible, to be left somehow holding the bag.

6

The cold knife of the wind slashed against Skye Fargo.

He fought the gusting mist of snow across the street to Puckett's Palace and swung inside. Hi Pocket, he noticed, had left the dust counter and was at a table in a corner, reading a tattered pink weekly. The customers were fewer in number but tougher in type. Drunken bravos, most heavily armed, guzzled rotgut and gambled, their voices rising raucous and boastful, a drunken trio singing ribald ditties at the bar. Fairly soon it would get so late or rowdy or both that the trading post would shutter.

Fargo elbowed through the gathering and in a moment stood facing the owner of the post.

Hi Pockets put down his paper, displeased. "What, you again?"

"Said I'd see you later," Fargo replied. "You, and Giles Nehalem."

"So you did. So what of it?"

"So it's this. I got jumped on the way here, over on the ridge."

Hi Pockets' surprise seemed genuine. "What happened?"

"One of the bushwhackers is back there dead. The other got clear."

"Listen, Fargo," Hi Pockets said earnestly, "I swear I didn't—"

"Somebody did. At the time I supposed they were just a pair of mangy outlaws. But now I figure somebody wasn't sure Eustace Chilton would quit without putting up a fight and wanted to make sure the odds were a little better."

For a moment they regarded each other evenly. Then Hi Pockets rose, folding his paper, and motioned for Fargo to follow. They headed straight for the poker games, passed the table Fargo had played at before, and came to the full table in the far corner.

Seated there was slab-bodied Modoc Thorne, next to a man who wore his hat slanted a little, shading his features. Although sitting hunched, the man was taller than Thorne and was massively proportioned; an opened blue jacket showed a white silk shirt and silver belt buckle.

There were also two brawny men in breeches, laced boots, and flannel shirts, looking similar to the laborer and blacksmith Fargo had played earlier, and a thin, sandy-bearded geezer wearing the clodhopper boots and coveralls of a farmer. Between the farmer and one of the laborers sat a man Fargo recognized from some place or another—Half-ear Teague, five-foot, crop-eared, and equally deadly with his knife or the twin pistols sagging in tied-down holsters.

They played out their round of stud. When one laborer won, the other laborer got up, conceding he'd been wiped clean, and Fargo sat down in his place. Hi Pockets pulled a spare chair up to the table and made a place for himself between Fargo and Half-ear Teague, which came as somewhat of a surprise to Fargo. Hi Pocket's own house rules forbade more than six to play, because in draw and deuces poker, with so many players the game was slowed by the need to shuffle in discards to fill out the draw. A slow game worked against the house because Hi Pockets took a fifty-cent cut per game. Of course, sitting in as a seventh player was his prerogative. But Fargo had a sneaking feeling that Hi Pockets had some profitable reason behind it as well.

Thorne gave Fargo a sidelong glance, grinning. "Thought you'd end up back here, Skye. Gone broke already or decided you wanted to be richer?"

Fargo chuckled. The big, tall man jerked, blurting, "Who? Skye who?"

Hi Pockets muttered, "He's him, Giles. Skye Fargo."

The man stared at Fargo. His cold gray eyes looked deceptively warm because of a flecking of red veins in the whites. His slicked-down hair gleamed, and though his lips had at some time been permanently scarred by someone's knuckles he was too proud to grow a covering mustache or beard. He struck Fargo as a man who would keep walking straight into punishment.

"Giles Nehalem, isn't it?" Fargo said, holding the man's stare without giving ground. "Understand you're ramrodding an express outfit."

"Territorial Director of Northern Overland, for your information."

"For my information, was it your nibs yourself I met on the ridge, or some flunky you sent?"

"I'm new here," Nehalem retorted. "I wouldn't

know what ridge you mean. Listen here, *Mister* Fargo, I've got a proposition I want to make to you."

Fargo tapped his revolver. "I've got one to make with this when I find the man I'm looking for, *Giles*."

"B'god, you're in for a trimming," Nehalem sneered angrily.

The laborers and the farmer looked puzzled, unaware of the situation. Thorne had some inkling and declared with gruff heartiness, "Yep, that's why we're gathered here, for a-trimmin' one another." He was shuffling the deck, since it was his turn. "Dealer's choice, but no oddball games. Take-out is twenty dollars in chips, but otherwise a player can play open, no limit. Let's see some stakes."

That hand was won by the same laborer. The game swayed around, no one winning or losing much, though Nehalem was shrewd and mostly won. He was by far the best player at the table, Fargo quickly determined, while the others could all be read as easily as the face of a card. The laborer sucked in his cheeks and frowned slightly when he got good cards. Similarly, the farmer drummed his fingers on the table. Half-ear Teague ordinarily held his cards in his left hand and bet with his right, but under stress he switched his cards to his right hand and bet with his left; this tipped Fargo not only to when he was going for a big pot, but also how he was apt to go for his guns.

"Well, I'll be a sonofabitch," Thorne said in disgust when Fargo caught him bluffing for the second time. He had yet to figure out what he was doing wrong. Nor did Hi Pockets catch on to his own habit of lighting and puffing on a cigar, pretending not to know when his turn came to bet; then after glancing around the table, he'd bet— a sure sign he had them.

Giles Nehalem dealt skillfully, a diamond as large as his thumbnail on his pinky finger sparkling in the artificial light. It took a few rounds of stud before Fargo detected a repetition in his actions: If the drawer helped his hand, Nehalem would quickly follow the deal as if to say nonchalantly, I got no help. Fargo could take as gospel that the last card had helped, though by how much was a stinker to gauge.

Having taken his time, some small losses, and made his judgments, Fargo settled down to play in earnest, with an emphasis on Nehalem. It began to have its effect, exacting a toll as the cards warmed and the bets mounted steadily.

The first really stiff tilt was a round of stud dealt by Nehalem. He lost two hundred bucks on three jacks against Fargo's three kings. Five minutes later Fargo raked in four hundred dollars on queens up, then followed up with a three-fifty pot that he bluffed on a pair of sixes. For a while the honors were even, each man holding his own. Yet Fargo had a feeling of impending disruption. And it wasn't long in coming.

What came was the lady.

She was blonde and somewhere close to thirty. Her body was lush, perhaps a couple of years past its prime, but her legs were exquisite and her full breasts and buttocks swelled her spangled green dress with sensual effect. Her eyes were blue and perky in a snub-nosed, slightly overpainted face, and a jeweled Spanish comb was set in her thick, upswept curls. She stopped in back of Nehalem's chair, and when she affectionately placed her hands on his shoulders, it was evident just whose lady she was.

"How's it going, Giles?" she asked him.

Nehalem said, "So-so," and because it happened to be his turn to deal again, he picked up the pack and began flipping out the hands for deuces wild.

From then on, the game was anything but so-so. Whatever else the lady was to Nehalem, she certainly wasn't his good-luck mascot. Despite his skill, he began to lose and kept on losing to everyone, even to the farmer, but mainly to Fargo.

It became an increasing strain to keep his poker face, and as time wore on, Nehalem began to growl out of the side of his mouth and to cheat whenever it was his turn to deal. The deck had a way of vanishing under the rim of the table or being spilled, face-up, by a convenient clumsy accident. And when he offered the pack to be cut, he always managed to replace the cut halves in the same order they had been in before the cut. It was amateur deck-stacking, but adept enough to avoid discovery by the other non-professional players. If Hi Pockets caught on, he studiously made no mention of it, and Half-ear Teague ignored it just like a good employee should.

Fargo was not particularly troubled by Nehalem's penchant for stacking the deck. The deal only came around to Nehalem once in every seven hands, and once Fargo had determined a pattern to Nehalem's tricks, he was able to work this against Nehalem and shift the odds accordingly. To his surprise, though, Nehalem didn't seem to need offsetting, his bad luck continuing with a vengeance.

It was as though the blonde lady's presence had jinxed Nehalem. She remained standing alongside, appearing bored, tired, as if her feet hurt, while he grew rigidly tensed, flushed, and furious. How well he cheated or how badly the others played didn't change his fortune, nor did the game the dealer chose, nor the fresh decks Nehalem demanded. He lost consistently and with each hand grew angrier, glowering whenever Fargo raked in another pot.

"Fargo," Nehalem finally growled "nobody can have your hellish luck."

Fargo's eyes were cold, and so was his smile. "Funny how losers call luck what winners call skill. Or are you thinking to call it otherwise, Giles?"

The other players paused, locked in their chairs, Thorne muttering under his breath, "Uh-oh, here we go again."

Nehalem gripped the table's edge, an accusation hanging on his lips, but he didn't utter it. Instead he sat rigid with frustration, snarling as Fargo stacked his chips. "I can't prove nothing, but take my advice. It ain't smart business to yank my horn."

"Glad to hear that's not the proposition you had in mind."

"Dammit, you know what I mean! Wise up, Fargo, you can't get Chilton's express to Portland. He hasn't the capital to push through a line of his own. Puckett tells me Chilton has built a reputation among the old-timers, but that's all he's got—just his name. I'll buy it for five hundred cash."

"I doubt he'd agree to sell."

"He doesn't, you can watch his routes being kicked apart."

"To Northern Overland, I reckon, it don't matter if his name stayed good or turned bad," Hi Pockets commented, hinting broadly. "Why, if that express pack of Chilton's was to never arrive and word leaked that his customers lost all what was theirs, well . . . Might be somebody could slip out of here, and no one the wiser, with a hefty stake in their pocket."

Fargo glared at Hi Pockets, feeling hot temper boil up into him again. Be companionable, don't try anything yet, he kept repeating to himself, as the laborer hurriedly declared, "L—let's play draw," and began dealing the cards. Watch it, Fargo told himself. Be companionable. This was no time or spot to let loose, not while he was hemmed in by Nehalem and Half-ear Teague along with Hi Pockets. Still, there was bite to his voice when Fargo asked Hi Pockets, "Are you in this mess so far you can't back out?"

Hi Pockets didn't answer, but his fingers tightened around his cigar, which had gone out.

"Take a long, hard look at your cards," Fargo said, picking up his hand. "This is going to be for blood."

They settled back into play. The better part of an hour passed, a longer time than Fargo had wanted to stay. He knew he couldn't leave as he had in the first game; it simply wasn't done unless a time limit was declared beforehand, especially when this had become somewhat of a grudge match. He was stuck until either he or Nehalem went bust, or he could instigate some excuse to quit.

His chance came fifteen minutes later. The deck passed to the farmer, who inserted the joker, re-shuffled, and awkwardly dealt five card draw, deuces wild. Everyone had something for openers, what with five wild cards, and betting grew steep before the draw. During the draw, Fargo asked for two cards, indicating he held a pair with a kicker or three of a kind, a comparatively weak hand that needed strong help from the draw.

The farmer was so nervous he could scarcely get a card off the top of the deck. Nehalem didn't help much by yelling at him to hurry up, goddamn it. The farmer finally flicked one card, then another facedown toward Fargo. The second touched Fargo's hand, bounced, then turned over, exposed.

It was the joker.

"I'm sorry," the farmer said, a deep pallor creeping over his weathered face. "What'll I do, Hi Pockets? Can't Fargo here take the joker?"

"Nope. If you'd read the rules you'd know a card exposed in the deal is a dead card. They're all printed and framed on the wall o'er there."

Stone-faced, Fargo showed no emotion. "It's okay. Give me another."

"Tough break," Nehalem jeered as the farmer dealt the next card to Fargo, and on his turn he took only one card, signaling he held a powerful pat hand.

Raises seesawed back and forth, Nehalem smirking with certain victory and Fargo apparently trying to make a poor bluff stick. The other players stayed in a while, but the betting soon got too rich for their taste, and one by one they folded their hands. It was between Nehalem and Fargo now, and the betting grew crazier. Finally, smug-faced and perspiring, Nehalem pushed the last of his reserves into the pot and said, "There, that's it."

"I'll match yours," Fargo said blithely, "and raise you five hundred more." He shoved his money forward. "Up to you, Giles."

"Take the five back," Nehalem snapped. "I was calling."

Fargo sat back, with an irritating grin of his own. "You didn't state a call, Giles. Besides, this is an open-ended game, isn't it?"

Nehalem looked ready to erupt. There wasn't a dime left in front of him, and if he didn't cough up five hundred, he'd forfeit the pot. The others stared breathlessly, waiting for him to do whatever he was going to do, Modoc Thorne groaning softly, "Here we go again, again." Eyeing Nehalem, Fargo wondered if this would be it, the provocation needed to blow the game. Nehalem considered his hand and then the pot, and asked Hi Pockets, "Will you cover me?"

Fargo expected Hi Pockets to capitulate, but the trader surprised him once more. "Let me tell y'all something," he replied, pointing at the rules on the wall. "I don't finance poker games. Particularly ones I'm playing in."

"You ain't risking nothing, goddamn it! I've got him beat!"

"Then beat him, Giles. Me, if I'd wanted to stay I'd have stayed and financed myself if I got into trouble. And another thing. You bastards slow the game. I only get fifty cents cut. This one I should cut fifty dollars."

Gritting teeth, Nehalem said to Fargo, "I'll have to give an IOU."

"You will in a pig's ass."

"Why, you—! What'll it take, collateral? Here, my ring—"

"Already won a diamond ring tonight. But, ah, how about the lady?"

Nehalem reared back, scowling. Sucking in her breath, the woman glanced uneasily from Nehalem to Fargo and back again. Fargo gave her a look as though appraising merchandise, then shrugged and threw another hundred onto the pile.

"My last offer, Giles. Now call or pitch in."

Nehalem rechecked his cards, then rubbed the back of his other hand across his mouth, his smoldering antagonism knifing into Fargo. But greed was heavier in his voice when he spat, "I'll call."

Fargo chuckled, though he actually found nothing funny about it. He eyed the woman, but saw no shock in her expression, no resentment or contempt. She merely appeared dismayed, sadly resigned to being treated like a possession. He felt sorry for her, but he was too deep in this clashing duel to give up the leverage she provided.

Fingers quivering, Nehalem spread out his cards. "Ten-high straight club flush," he announced. "And I did it by drawing a deuce. Who says my luck's sour?" Chortling, he made a pass to rake in the pot.

Fargo's fist reached out and almost broke Nehalem's wrist. "Hands off!"

"It's mine, you prick!"

"Not yet," Fargo said evenly, and laid his cards down one at a time. "I was dealt a deuce, then drew another after the joker. Didn't give me a flush, only a full house, treys full. These three treys . . . plus this pair of treys."

"*Five* threes?" Nehalem roared, half choking. "Lousy *threes*?"

Fargo nodded, grinning. Hi Pockets swore in amazement; Half-ear Teague grunted, shifting his chair away expectantly as he saw Nehalem slowly rising, his features congealing with rage and hatred.

Ignoring Nehalem, Fargo began gathering his winnings.

"It stinks." Nehalem leaned forward, half up out

of his chair, smarting with fury and the need to redeem himself. "Leave that pot lay, you!"

A strange hush descended about the table. The lady rubbed her palms along the thighs of her dress, looking embarrassed and distressed. Some players at the adjoining tables swiveled to stare, sensing the brewing confrontation. Fargo alone seemed unaware—or unconcerned. He continued loading his pockets, watching the money instead of Nehalem.

"What's the matter, you deaf?" Nehalem shoved his chair back and stood hovering, his polished fingernails glinting in the lamplight as he eased his hand toward the waist of his open jacket. "Don't touch no more, and dump the loot you've taken back on the table."

Fargo glanced up, unperturbed. "You talking to me, Giles?"

"I'm calling you."

The lady laughed once, sharply, out of nervousness. That was the only sound as the hush spread, more men pausing to watch. Fargo shifted slightly, checking around for signs of jiggers ready to side Nehalem, but didn't spot any in particular other than Half-ear Teague. The short gunman watched unmoving, unblinking, a trained viper awaiting word to strike. Modoc Thorne gazed about, arms crooked casually over his revolver butt as though resting on it for support. The farmer and laborer were tense statues, swallowing thickly. Only Hi Pockets was showing any agitation, lurching against the table as he reared ponderously from his seat, blustering, "Keep peaceable, boys, calm down or get out. No fighting allowed in my joint. Hear me, Fargo? No more brawling."

Fargo stared at Nehalem. "Then call me by my

name, Giles." He grinned ferally, scooping another wad of money into his pockets.

"The cheat's pulling a gun!" Nehalem yelled treacherously, to save face while he reached for his own hideout pistol.

Fargo lunged upright, his legs tilting the table on edge. He struck Nehalem with a straight-armed fist to the nose as the table fell over, spilling money and cards. Nehalem stumbled backward and tripped against his chair, blood spurting from his mashed nose. He triggered reflexively, his howl of pain lost in the blast of his half-drawn Sharps .32 "stingy gun," its bullet skewing downward and plowing at an angle through the table.

Fargo was already launching around the other side of the table, casting a fleeting glance at Half-ear Teague. Teague was uncoiling into action, darting at a tangent to catch Fargo in a crossfire, the commotion and upended table momentarily stymieing him from a clear bead. The immediate threat was Nehalem, who was training his small pistol for a second point-blank shot. He was swift, but not swift enough. Swerving, Fargo plunged across the littered gap, closing too fast, too soon to haul his revolver to bear, diving at Nehalem with fists pistoning before the man shifted aim and triggered. Fargo pummeled him with a combination of punches, right and left belts to his gut and solar plexus, and drubbing jabs to his heart. Nehalem started tumbling over his chair, arms windmilling, pistol flying from nerveless fingers. Pressing, Fargo battered Nehalem furiously in a driving rush to drop him cold and quick—damn quick. Half-ear Teague was storming through the crowd, mere seconds away, guns drawn.

Teetering, both eyes swollen shut, Nehalem tried to fight back. But Fargo ducked under the swings and walloped him in the belly and face, pinning him against the upended table. Dazed and bleeding, Nehalem sagged to his knees, bewildered by the relentless savagery of Fargo's assault. Fargo brought his right fist up from somewhere down around his boots. It hit Nehalem's chin with the sound heard in a slaughterhouse, when a steer was brained with a maul. Nehalem arched sideward, stumbling, entangled in the chair and collapsed to the floor so hard that he snapped off all four legs.

And there Giles Nehalem lay, flat out.

Fargo heard the running tap of footsteps, and, suspecting Half-ear Teague, stabbed for his revolver while swinging about in a crouch. But it was just the lady, coming to look at Nehalem; she jerked to a halt, gasping, startled as he spun, readying to shoot. Lips quirked wryly, he pivoted on around in search of One-ear Teague, telling her brusquely:

"Keep back. Nehalem's okay, so stay away, back out of range—"

A bullet whistled past Fargo's cheek, its breath hot and vicious so closely did it singe his skin. The blasting report rang in his ears as Fargo whirled, scanning, pluming gunsmoke marking the shot but masking who had fired. One-ear Teague, he bet, who'd fire and flee, scouting his next shot, hidden in this chaos of drunks clamoring and the lady screaming. Still wheeling, knowing he was wide-open here, Fargo cut and headed for cover. As he dashed toward the upended table, a bullet singed the air next to the skin of his neck. He sprang aside, then threw himself to the grungy floorboards and crawled on elbows and knees as pursuing slugs shrieked through the broken furniture, clipping wood and fabric in a whining fury.

Scrambling, Fargo rolled in behind the table, which rested on its side with its thick wooden top upright like a shield. Rapidly he checked his revolver loads while lead snarled and ripped above and aside him, or punched into the table top with sickening crunches. He couldn't afford to remain here behind cover because nobody seemed willing or able to bring Half-ear Teague to bay, meaning help was never coming, while Teague had unopposed rein to strafe or attack any time or way, or to circle around and snake in on Fargo from behind.

So clenching his teeth, Fargo hunched low and darted out. It was simple. The plain-furnished, open room yielded meager cover, and what there was now was swamped in utter bedlam. Along the rear, near where Fargo stood, folks were scrambling away and mobbing frontward, carrying on worse than a stockyard stampede. Just as well, though, it got them out of line of fire, gave him space to maneuver, and left Half-ear Teague exposed. No hiding now, no scheming, no tricky bullshit, just run and shoot.

Fargo ran with bullets whistling after him. They smashed into the walls and furnishings but none tagged him. And he shot, the Colt blazing in his fist while he dodged lead, his snapshots missing Half-ear Teague. In response, Teague triggered swiftly—too swiftly, his bullets straying wide.

Ignoring it, Fargo kept on coming. Teague, face virulently contorted, began advancing on Fargo as though goaded into taking up a dare, his yellowed bone-handled revolvers blasting through blinding billows of powdersmoke. The smoke probably saved his life, Fargo reckoned, spoiling Teague's aim as well as his own. He felt a motion ahead—an impression rather than a distinct sight—of a savage rush and the glint of a revolver. Teague was angling his revolvers around to bear, and Fargo was hastily leveling his Colt for a shot when both men triggered reflexively. One was the barest echo to the other and for the next few instants it was impossible to tell whose gun had roared first.

Both men stood upright, smoke curling out of the long barrels of their revolvers. Then the weapon in Teague's right hand dipped a little. His shoulders sagged and he took a step ahead, but suddenly there was water in his legs and he went down hard on his knees. The jolt unsettled his revolver and it slipped from his fingers. Teague started to bend forward, then he caught himself. With an effort he brought his head back up and the revolver in his left hand lifted.

Fargo fired again.

This slug caught Teague in the chest and hurled him back. He landed on his side with his left arm under him. His straining, gaping mouth was plain to every man in the Palace. Still watching warily, Fargo knew the shootout had been a toss-up, a split whisker that could have fallen either way, although the odds had been stacked heavily against him. His hunch had played out, though—the gunman plied his trade as he played his cards, favoring his left when under stress. Knowing his opponent's habits, anticipating his probable leanings and leadings, had given Fargo a killing edge. Half-ear Teague kicked twice and then rolled over on his stomach. He did not move after that.

Fargo whirled, eyes scanning the room for more

trouble. The hullabaloo had eased to a dull bab-
bling, though a number were hooting and the lady
was whimpering. Hi Pockets glared at Fargo while
haranguing for volunteers and bribing a few with
whiskey to cart off the deceased.

Thorne came over, smiling. "Great show. Sloppy,
but successful."

"Well, ain't that dandy. Where were you when I
needed help?"

"I'm not sure. I didn't know you were in any
trouble."

Fargo stared at Thorne, wondering whether to
believe him. Thorne looked like he'd told the truth
about that, and about everything else he'd ever
done in his angelic life, his eyes fairly weeping with
sincerity. He must be lying.

Hi Pockets pushed pugnaciously up to Fargo then,
hands fisted on his hips. "I warned you! No fighting
and no killing, dammit, them's the rules!"

The farmer horned in, starting, "He was only
defending—"

But he was cut off by Fargo, who countered, "I
was called out, and called a cheat. Giles Nehalem
can't get away with calling me a cheat."

"Well, maybe you are. For certain you're a trou-
blemaker and rabble-rouser. Maybe I ought to send
for my bouncers."

"Damrow and Trent?" Fargo chuckled. "Fat lot
of good they'll do you. I'm going now."

"Yeah? And what about the damage you caused?"

"Pay it out of my damn winnings left on the
floor," Fargo replied, turning to stride toward the
door. "Squeeze any more that you need out of
your buddy on the floor. Nehalem can afford to
cover what he starts."

Thorne called, "Not so fast, Skye, you're forgetting your lassie."

Hesitating, Fargo glanced back at Nehalem's lady. There was pleading in her eyes, and a barely perceptible pulse to her breast. "Nope, she's not with me," he replied affably, and was turning to head for the door again when Modoc Thorne stuck it to him:

"Such chivalry, Skye. It's plumb inspiring. But the fact remains you won her, and leaving her behind is same as leaving your winnings on the floor." Turning toward Hi Pockets, Thorne smiled and talked on, "Rule is, it all goes to you. Stick to your rules this time, Hi. Don't dicker. All the money he dropped and the snookums he dumped is yours!"

"Snookums?" Puckett reared as if scalded. "A gal? Send her off!"

"Hi, your rule states all winnings left undeclared are forfeited to the house. Meaning to you, you sly hound, explicitly, with no exceptions."

Puckett fumed, "Don't be absurd!" Thrusting toward Fargo, he raged, "From here on, rules is no left women allowed! You won her, you take her, and quit trying to foist 'em on me! Women with me is taboo!"

Any doubt Fargo may have had that Thorne had set him up vanished when he heard Thorne's phony commiseration with Puckett. "You got it right, Hi, women is women. Some men says women is a necessary evil, like hooch, African dominoes, an' castor oil. I try to do without 'em all . . ."

The lady caught up to him then. "You got me," she said with a shrug, and added as they began moving for the door, "Sorry. I didn't want you to get stuck with me, and I know you must be disappointed. I'll keep from underfoot."

"You got it wrong," Fargo replied gruffly. "I didn't want Nehalem to take it out on you, and he couldn't, so long as you're not with me."

"Well, I'm not with Giles either." She plucked at her green dress. "I won't go back with him, and even if I wanted to, I don't believe he'd let me."

Fargo opened the front door, and as the woman swept outside, Hi Pockets yelled at him, "Nehalem will kill you for all this, Fargo. Him and his crew. I'm telling you, get out while you can, and don't come back!"

"Can't yet, Hi. I got to see you again about the pack, don't forget." Fargo stepped outside and slammed the door.

7

Rose Burleigh was her name.

"Wild Rose," she asserted, "not the domesticated type." That was all she said while accompanying Fargo across to the hotel, cuddling close against him and shivering from the cold. The wind had died, thankfully, the brief gusty front having rushed on, leaving the night deep and still. The air was frigid and a little damp, yet it was fresh after the stuffy interior of Puckett's trading post.

When they entered the lobby, the fat woman at the counter fluttered her eyes open and growled, "Just where do you think you're traipsing?"

"Why, to sign in," Fargo hastened to reply. "The lady needs a room."

Humphing, the fat woman took money from Fargo and gave Rose a key. "Room Twelve, upstairs. At the tuther end of the hall from Twenty-two," she added pointedly. "I trust the accommodations will stay at that distance."

Rose smiled as they climbed the stairs. "Trusting cow, isn't she?"

Again, that was all she said. Nor did Fargo question. He'd known too many women like her, from rich men's baggage to *cantina conchitas,* not to recognize that her business was pleasure and her pleasure was business. On the whole, he enjoyed her sort. They didn't fool with that society-belle-virgin routine of coyness and teasing. When they liked you, they showed it, and when they didn't, they ended it. Their past was a dead issue, best left buried.

Reaching her room first, she unlocked the door and beckoned him inside. "Light the lamp for me, will you? I don't have any matches."

It took Fargo a few moments to grope through the darkness and locate the lamp. Firing the wick, he heard Rose shut the door behind him, and then a murmuring swell of voices rising from the street. Peeking out through the side of the drawn window shade, he saw that Hi Pockets had closed for the night, his patrons dispersing along the street as the proprietor padlocked the front door.

Rose said, "I relax better with my clothes off."

Turning from the window, Fargo saw that her dress was heaped carelessly on the floor. Her arms were crossed, and she was removing her lace-trimmed shift, exposing creamy smooth skin and plumply quivering, cherry-tipped breasts.

"C'mon, sport, what're you waiting for?" she teased, untying the strings of her drawers.

Fargo grinned lustily. "Later. I got to see someone in half an hour."

"Well, then, hurry up. Let's not waste it." She slid down her drawers and stepped out of them, along with her high-button shoes. Her body was pale, although slightly freckled, and Fargo saw that she was naturally blonde, a fringe of downy curls accentuating her rounded pink nether lips.

"You're staring," she purred, padding nearer.

"Don't be shy, you can touch me. I'm yours to touch, aren't I?"

Fargo leaned forward and kissed the jutting red peaks of her breasts. She moaned, pressing close, and he ran his hand down along her flat belly and into her golden fleece. He felt her fingers unbuttoning his fly, dipping in and grasping his erect member, stroking him sensuously, releasing him only long enough for him to strip naked and then leading him to the bed.

Fargo pulled her to him by the waist and lowered her onto the coverlet. He crawled in alongside her, kissing her breasts again, suckling her nipples while his hands parted her sensitive loins, his fingers caressing, massaging as he eased his way inside her. Wild Rose Burleigh sighed and mewed with growing arousal, her body undulating against him, her own hand slipping between them to rub and fondle him.

"Now, sport," she panted, "do it now . . ."

Rising, Fargo knelt over her. She lay silent with anticipation, her legs spread on either side of him, her exposed pink furrow moist and throbbing. He levered downward, and she gasped with the rock-hard feel of him as he began his spearing entry. She pushed upward, her thighs clasping him, swallowing his thick meaty length up inside her.

"Lordy, lordy," she moaned, her muscles squeezed around him so tightly that Fargo nearly cried out with pleasure. He thrust, and she automatically responded in rhythm, mewling deep in her throat, her splayed thighs arching spasmodically against his pumping hips.

He started a slow, easy tempo, and slid his hands down to cup her jiggling buttocks. He licked her cheek, and laved her ear with his tongue, feeling her warm breath pulsing in his own ear. Then their mouths touched, pressing together with lips apart and tongues curling. Their pace increased, and increased again, their passion mounting greedily.

Soon their rhythm grew frenzied. She rolled him over, he rolled her over, back and forth, their nude bodies frantic in their pounding madness. Fargo's breath rasped in his throat; Rose's legs clamped where they gripped his middle. There was nothing but exquisite sensation, no existence beyond the boundaries of their flesh.

Rose squealed as her climax struck. Her nails raked Fargo's back with each spasm, her limbs jerking violently. Fargo felt his own swift orgasm, his juices spewing hotly into her. She absorbed all of his flowing passion, until, in a final convulsion, she lay still, satiated.

"Never with Giles," she sighed blissfully. "Never like that."

After a moment, Fargo withdrew gently and stretched out beside her. He remained silent for a while, his hand resting on her thigh.

At last he got up and put his clothes back on. Placing a thick bundle of currency on the bureau, he gazed over at Rose, who was half-dozing on the rumpled coverlet. "Here's a split of my winnings from Nehalem."

"Keep it." She sounded hurt. "I wasn't selling."

"I'm not buying. Nehalem is; he's buying you a going-away present to wherever you want, to do whatever you want. Take it as it's meant."

Rose nodded, her eyes misting, and started to say something, when her words were lost in an explosive roar. The eruption came from outside the hotel, and though a bit muffled, it was a window-rattling, timber-quivering shock of a blast.

"Stay here," Fargo cautioned, leaping for the door.

When he reached the street, Fargo was engulfed by people boiling from all directions, all yelling and gesticulating. Plumes of black smoke wreathed Puckett's Palace. Shoving and bellowing, Hi Pockets plowed through the crush toward his trading post, Fargo and others following right behind.

A moment more and they were before the building entrance. Its heavy front door and small-paned windows were all blown out, and black powdersmoke percolated from their shattered frames. With Puckett leading, they plunged through the entrance into the wreckage of the one big room.

They halted, Puckett cursing between spasms of coughing as they peered around the pungent, murky gloom. Tables and chairs were reduced to kindling, and even the massive plank counter was toppled over. In the far corner stood the safe, its ponderous steel door lying on the floor, its dark interior gaping like an eyeless socket.

They made their way to the safe, already knowing what they'd find. "Nothing!" Puckett raged, squinting into it. "It's been cleaned. But there weren't no reason to set powder to everything else. The bastards blew up my joint for the hell of it."

"Or because they didn't know how to handle powder," Fargo suggested. "How much was lost?"

"Whatever Chilton's express was worth, I reckon. There were pretty slim pickings in there tonight except for the pack. The robbers picked the wrong night." Puckett grinned maliciously at Fargo. "Or I guess maybe it was the right night, depending how you look at it."

They hastened back outside. Puckett called to the milling group, asking if anyone had seen the culprits. An excited miner stumbled forward. "Saw one jasper, smack on the heels of the blast, hightailing it on horseback from around back of here and up the street."

It flashed through Fargo's mind that pursuit would be easy. A horse had but two avenues of escape in that direction—north over the mountains to a mountain valley known as Excelsior, or east along the trail he'd taken here. Mountains hemmed the region on all sides. A lone robber might escape if he were strong and a mountain climber, but he couldn't pack sufficient food to last through, much less the express pack.

"With luck we can run him down," Fargo declared.

"We?" Puckett sneered. "It's your—"

A burst of gunshots and a yelping howl sounded from up the street. It was followed almost instantly by confused shouts and tramping boots as two men pounded hurriedly from the mouth of an alleyway up by the livery stable.

"Now what's busted loose?" Puckett barked, starting for the alley. Fargo and the others sprinted along with him, converging on the two men and bunching around.

"We was at the river dock," one of the men reported breathlessly. "All of a sudden, this big sonofabitch races at us, shooting. We hit snow, let me tell you, and he jumps in a canoe and shoves off."

"The robber switched to a canoe!" Puckett said.

"He must have figured he'd be ridden down in a chase."

"A horse can make faster time downstream than a canoe," Fargo asserted, and dashed to the nearby stable. Modoc Thorne, he suddenly noticed, was at his heels, shouting. "What is it, Thorne?" he called back.

"I've got a canoe. Let's take it and follow," Thorne suggested.

Fargo paused, his hand on his Ovaro's neck. The horse was wet and lathered. Someone had ridden it while he'd been at Puckett's and the hotel, and ridden it hard. Tough as the Ovaro was, it was in no shape for a long, hard pursuit. And now the canvas-coated man was offering to take him for a ride on the river. Well, that might give him the answer . . .

"Okay, get out your canoe," Fargo replied.

The two men carried the canoe from the rear of the livery stable barn down a crooked path to a crudely built landing that jutted into the Snake River. Thorne had included a couple of '52 Enfield .577 rifles he said he'd just had "lying around" along with powder and shot. Launching the canoe, Fargo took the bow paddle and placed the rifle given him within easy reach as the river carried them swiftly away.

Swiftly they rode the winding currents toward the brutally wild beginnings of Hells Canyon. Now and then the pale wash from a half-moon flowed along with them, highlighting the river's sharp twists and turns. But often as not, churning, thick clouds blanketed the sky, darkly forecasting another storm.

Fargo sent the canoe into the fastest water and over small falls, figuring the pursued canoe would take the slower, safer water. Each slight gain counted.

A half hour passed without incident, then he saw the other canoe. Almost at the same instant, one of the two men in the canoe ahead saw them, and whipped the canoe into a raging torrent.

"I thought there was only one crook," Thorne called to him.

"That's what was seen," Fargo allowed. "Maybe one stayed with the boat."

"Doesn't make sense, but they're foolish. They'll capsize in that water."

"No, they won't. They're carrying ballast in the bottom of their canoe—express pack ballast," Fargo countered. "Send me into quieter water."

He dropped his paddle and opened fire as soon as the canoe steadied. His lead must have gone close, he reasoned, because the man in the bow dropped his paddle, caught up a rifle, and returned the fire.

"Come on, Thorne," Fargo shouted, "let's close in on 'em. This rough water will keep us bobbing around so there's not much danger that they'll hit us." He picked up the paddle and began driving ahead.

A few minutes later he picked up the rifle again, loaded, and fired. A geyser leaped up at the water line. "That ball drilled their canoe," Fargo shouted, hurriedly reloading. "One more should put 'em in a mood to quit." He aimed again. Just as he was about to pull the trigger, the canoe swerved violently. An instant later he and Modoc Thorne were struggling in the current, so cold that it slammed the breath out of Fargo's lungs.

"Hit a snag!" Thorne shouted.

"Can you make it?" Fargo asked. "Swim with the current and we'll make that bar downstream."

"I'll be alright," Thorne answered, striking out for the bank.

The other canoe vanished around a point downstream. Fargo struggled shoreward, choking and spent when he stumbled up onto the snowy bank. Making sure that Thorne was safe, he broke into a steady trot back toward Lewiston, aware he had to keep moving to keep warm. And to keep his hands busy and his mind off the chill, he tackled the problem of drying his revolver while he ran, replacing caps and charges from the waterproof powder cannister Thorne had given him with the rifle.

The damp smell of the river became heavy with rot and mud and garbage as Fargo reached the town. Ahead stretched a series of rickety docks and landings, which he skirted by angling up the bank toward the structures lining the street. He dove along one of the narrow passages between buildings— when suddenly black outlines took shape in the street ahead.

The figures were dark blurs in the murky dimness in the passageway. Instinctively Fargo flattened against the side of the building, and an instant later the distorted shadows of two horsemen in round-brimmed felt hats and Conestoga boots writhed against the background of log and unpainted plank walls. Gunflame speared at him, the riders storming down the passageway in single file, their bullets shattering wood and hardpan.

Fargo fired twice at the first rider. One slug tore through the man's coat, nicking his ribs, but the second slug knocked him off his horse as if he'd been hit with a heavy club. The man fell under the chopping hoofs of the second horse, screaming, tripping the horse off-stride and almost dumping the second rider. Echoes crashed against the close-set walls of the buildings as the second rider and Fargo shot at each other and missed. Fargo felt the breath of one bullet just before he sprang aside, the second rider galloping on with raking spurs, he and the first horse racing out from the rear of the passage and veering upriver, hoofbeats fading swiftly into the night.

When there was no longer the slightest sound, Fargo stepped out to the fallen gunman, who was groveling, panting curses, twitching feebly on the ground. The Trailsman struck a match, kneeling over the man to see if he could recognize him. He couldn't.

"You came all this way to die in an alley," Fargo said softly. "You're a damn idiot, friend."

The mist of death was stealing over the man's eyes, obscuring them. "Fuck you," he mumbled, and said no more.

Fargo played the light around the man for a moment before the match burnt itself out. The only thing of interest he glimpsed were the hoofprints churned in the frigid earth. One of the gunmen had been riding a pigeon-toed horse with worn shoes.

Fargo headed to the street, and stopped by Puckett's Palace on his way to the hotel. Hi Pockets was inside his bombed trading post, cleaning up the worst of the mess with the help of several men— including his bouncers, Damrow and Trent, and a sobered Joel Dumas.

After Fargo briefly related what had happened, Puckett asked, "You say Thorne upset the canoe just as you was about to get in the finishing shot?"

"I said the canoe struck a snag and upset."

"Damned funny Thorne couldn't have steered

the canoe clear of the snag," Puckett observed. "It seems to me maybe you won't have to look very far for one of the heisters."

"That's mighty thin, Hi Pockets. Doesn't prove a thing," Fargo objected. Yet it was food for thought, he had to admit, along with the fact that Modoc Thorne was the only man he knew who could have approached his Ovaro, and the horse had been all a-lather. Still . . . "Let's not jump to conclusions."

"Certainly," Puckett agreed. "Now, mind you, I don't think Thorne would be fool enough to take an actual part in the robbery. But he was here till I closed, and he'd know when to strike. And for a cut in the loot, he might clear the path of obstacles. But it's up to you, Fargo, makes little difference to me." Puckett smiled cynically. "I'll make my loss back easy enough, 'cause folks will always drink and gamble and make hogs of themselves. But the only way you'll recover Chilton's express is to track the dogs down."

Fargo stared at Puckett, sensing derision in the depths of his eyes. On that note, he walked out of the trading post, hotel-bound to change his clothes. As he was crossing the street, he heard his name called and saw Joel Dumas rushing to catch up. Fargo nodded curtly with no friendly overtures.

"Listen, Fargo," Dumas said, "I'd like to buy that ring back."

"Why?"

"Well, I'd just like to. I've got the hundred dollars with me."

"What makes you think I'd take a hundred bucks?"

Dumas's eyes clouded and he bit his lip for a moment. "Well, I thought you'd take a hundred, seeing as I paid you a hundred."

"That's not how it works. By the way, where'd you scrounge a hundred?"

"I—I—well, I don't see—"

"As it's any of my business." Fargo paused, frowning, then said, "I've been around a bit, and've gotten to know a few things about stones. Now, I'm curious to know why you're willing to pay me a hundred dollars for an imitation diamond that's worth maybe ten dollars, if that."

Joel Dumas opened his mouth to say something, but closed it again sharply and ground one mittened hand in the palm of the other, while his eyes darted about evasively.

"Tell me why, Dumas," Fargo pursued.

"I—I, well, I always thought it was genuine."

"I don't mind telling you that I think you're lying. At any rate, I paid you the hundred dollars on a whim, and to give you a last chance for a comeback. Now it's my whim to not sell the ring back to a liar."

Dumas stood, his hands clenched, his lower lip quivering. Then he pivoted and tramped off to Puckett's Palace.

Fargo continued on toward the hotel. Lewiston was becoming a deadly, desperate mining camp, but that was to be expected, he supposed. Violence went hand in hand with inordinate ambition, and the big rainbow held the tinge of blood as well as the mythical pot of gold. Young Joel Dumas had not learned that yet. Skye Fargo had learned it too well, and was tired of it. No doubt plenty more lay in store before things were settled.

Then Fargo grew aware that somebody was stalking him.

To made certain, he walked past the hotel and

turned idly along a narrow and meandering side lane lined by canvas tents. A short distance along he came to a bouldered outcrop, and turned amongst the huge rocks and waited. Very soon he heard the scrape of boots, then the hulking figure of Damrow passed. It was a patch of white he noticed first, actually, Damrow's nose taped up with bandages.

Fargo stroked his bearded jaw thoughtfully as the boot falls receded, then slipped off in another direction and circled back to the hotel. Rousing the fat woman to retrieve his parcel from her safe, he took it upstairs with gun in hand. His door rested unlocked, loose on its latch. Entering cautiously, he discovered the room ransacked. His belongings had been rifled, the furnishings pulled apart, the mattress slit with its batting strewn.

Hastily clearing up and donning dry duds, Fargo left the room in a peevish temper. His stuff had been strewn but not stolen. Not a thing seemed to be missing—except for any trace of who had done it or why. Joel Dumas perhaps, seeking his ring, or Nehalem hunting personal secrets and confidences. Or it could have just been a sneak-thief scum looting for the dust poke now in his pocket. After all, that transaction in the dining room had been witnessed. In any case, he was definitely late to meet Amity, and determined to learn more about this skunkhole mess.

8

Quickly and quietly Skye Fargo padded downstairs, careful not to disturb the dozing fat woman as he crossed the lobby and headed along the main floor hall.

At Number Nine he paused, hearing a man's loud laugh coming from some room farther on. He rapped softly and waited, then rapped again. There was no response. He tried the door knob and it turned, so he eased into the darkened room, not wanting to be spotted there in the corridor. He caught the scent of fresh tobacco smoke mingling with the scent of lilac water.

Then something hard jabbed into his back, and a gutteral voice mumbled, "I know you've got it, kiddo, so hand it over."

Fargo halted. The one window dimly highlighted a stand with a water pitcher, but nothing more. He caught the sound of breathing, and the scent of lilac water was still in the room. But it was the man's voice, one that he had heard before but could not quite identify at the moment.

Fargo kept his voice calm. "Reach in my pocket, mister. It looks like I played the sucker."

A hand groped at his side. Fargo clutched it in a viselike grip and, wheeling around, jerked the arm over his shoulder, bending and heaving. A form went over him and crashed on the floor, and Fargo was surprised that the gun in his short-ribs had not exploded. He spun toward the door, when a match flared and a woman's tight voice said, "Excellent, Mr. Fargo. Wait a minute."

Fargo turned slowly, his mouth open. The girl calmly removed the glass chimney from the table lamp and applied the match to its wick. By its yellow glow he saw Amity Dumas smiling as she looked up from the lamp. A man climbed up from the floor, letting out a deep breath. Fargo stared at him.

"Modoc Thorne! Do you regularly stick up folks in dark hotel rooms, or'd you hightail back here special to gun me down?"

Still in wet clothes, a sour grin on his face, Thorne gestured with a blackened briar pipe. "That was my pipestem in your ribs, Skye. I'd of been the one killed if Amity hadn't struck a light, 'cept now if I don't catch my death of cold, it'll be a wonder." He wagged his pipe at the girl. "You satisfied?"

"Satisfied so far," Amity conceded, regarding Fargo attentively. "You have my dust poke, I expect, or you wouldn't have tackled Modoc like that." Fargo handed it over, and she unsealed and emptied it on the table. It was black sand. "Sorry to play a trick on you, but it's not a joke. I need help. Modoc says you'll do, from what he's seen, but I had to make sure. At stake is a small fortune in gold dust that I'm anxious to get out."

Guardedly Fargo smiled. "I'm a poor risk, as Thorne knows and should've made clear. I couldn't even get through with the load I packed in, ma'am—"

"Call me Amity, please."

"Call me Skye, then. But by all means, if your brother's made any money, you're smart to try shipping it away. Leave it here with him, Amity, and somebody'll take it and his life, too."

"Joel's through here, Mr.—Skye. We're orphans, and we scrimped long and hard for his grubstake. He did strike it rich, only it's gone to his wits, like he just can't get used to not being poor anymore. Modoc took kindly and tried to keep a weather eye on Joel, but he finally sent for me. Now we've prevailed on Joel to sell the claim and return to Portland with me."

Fargo glanced at Thorne. "Sell to who?"

"Hi Pockets. He brokers as a sideline. It's his buy-out money Amity's talking about. Joel's blown all the dust he panned."

"I have it right here." Amity turned toward a small cowhide trunk and opened the lid, revealing stacks of gold-filled parfleches. "Mr. Puckett was so anxious to deal a fair shake, he paid more than Modoc thinks the claim's actually worth."

"Hi Pockets always pays top dollar for what he wants," Thorne commented, tamping tobacco into his pipe. "Well, I reckon he can afford it, seeing he gets it all back again, out on the trails somewheres."

"Smell a rat, do you?"

"For some while now. He's set himself up with that glossy reputation, but he's got a streak as cold as a dead carp in his eyes." Thorne sparked a match on his boot sole and fired his pipe, adding as he puffed, "Clearly there's a tipoff man here in town. Men don't get robbed on the trail into town. It's always someone toting his payload out. I suspect Hi

Pockets points the finger and one of his toadies passes word to the contact outside."

"And certainly there must be other outlaw informers snooping about," Amity put in. "My plan was to draw you here for a talk without anyone knowing it. You came to Lewiston with a pack train, a total stranger. Everybody knows you'll be leaving town empty-handed tomorrow, not worth hijacking. Taking my dust along would be simple."

"Simpleminded," Fargo retorted—then paused, staring. The sight of Modoc Thorne wreathed in pipe smoke awoke the memory of a kindred likeness. "Briar!" he exclaimed, snapping his fingers. "Briar Thorne!"

Modoc bridled. "I'm his son," he growled, clipping his words. "Now go ahead, give me funny looks. Sure, my old man bossed an outlaw gang workin' out of the Hole years ago. But he served his time and paid his law debt, and that squares accounts. 'Sides, I'm not to blame, I can't help what Bandit Briar Thorne done."

"Yeah, we can't pick our kin," Fargo agreed, and let it drop, picking up again with Amity, "You're kidding yourself to think I'll be going ignored and running the trails unhassled. If Hi Pockets aims to get your gold, he aims to get my winnings. Giles Nehalem is also going to be out for revenge, and I'm sure he'll have a bushwhacker after me. That's just for starters. Your setup doesn't need me along drawing more trouble."

"It seems like I put the saddle on the wrong horse," Amity admitted, disappointed. "It puts us right back before, dancing on hot coals. Joel's made such a rowdy display, I'm afraid for us to take the dust out. Modoc would attract attention because he doesn't go out often and everybody knows he's befriended us. There's nobody else to help, leastwise none I'd trust, and I'd rather not repeat my hoax. I wish you'd figure some way, somehow or other, I'm not too picky. If you're interested, it'll be worth your while."

About to refuse her offer, Fargo held his tongue. He still could feel an odd gut feeling, an intuition that Modoc Thorne might well be his canvas-coated gunman. This son of Bandit Briar had been damn eager to go along with him on the trip down the river; now Thorne was acting Amity's protector and Fargo's pal. And that made Fargo think with some regret of Amity fighting against killers, her gold-crazy brother, and perhaps even Modoc Thorne. She had courage, that girl. She deserved better than to die trying to run her gold out, slaughtered by outlaw bullets or butchered by treachery.

Inwardly cursing himself for a soft-soaped idiot, Fargo told Amity, "Well, I've got a bone to pick with the same general bunch that you're up against. I doubt Hi Pockets blew up his place to hash safe-cracking himself, but if I'm to get back the express pack, I wouldn't doubt I'll have to cross him to do it. Who knows, Amity, I may eliminate your problem solving my own."

"Or find worse ones," Thorne countered darkly. "Do you aim to scout out far on your own?"

"Far as it takes to find the pack."

"Riding out is more a two-man job now, no news to you. If you want help, I'll go along."

"I'll remember. And I'll look you up when I find the pack," Fargo said, turning to Amity. "Likely we can talk a deal. Meantime, it's better nobody realizes we're on the same side. And move your gold. Your window and door aren't worth the pain of locking them, and you can bet that Joel and Hi Pockets can't be trusted not to talk about the sale. Somebody might just break right in and remove the gold for you. So hide it someplace safe, someplace else. Otherwise, I'll be worried about you."

Amity held out her hand, and as Fargo felt its warm smallness in his callused palm, she said, "We'll be alright, but I'm glad to know that you will." And she smiled up at him, her lustrous eyes darkening to mulberry smoke.

When Fargo was out of Room Nine and padding upstairs again, his thoughts strayed to Briar Thorne. He'd never met the old desperado, but for a while it seemed Briar was in every gazette and wanted poster, and it was from the same old line-cut illustration they all seemed to borrow that Briar's likeness had become engrained in Fargo's memory. From most all accounts, Briar was a smart lobo. He had originally located in Jackson Hole, where terrain and weather sorely tried attempts to root him out. When things finally became too hot for Briar Thorne and his men, they slipped away and began looking for another hideout.

Eventually they found Excelsior. It offered a natural defense of mountain barriers, and much of the time deep snows frustrated authorities' attempts to penetrate the region. There was a valley of good graze where they could grow vegetables, run enough cattle to satisfy their needs, and have ample wood for buildings and fuel. The Briar Thorne gang raided what few placer camps were around, and preyed on travelers along the rivers and the Oregon and Lewis and Clarke trails. They thrived until the army garrison at Fort Walla Walla and a whole passel of local lawmen, after considerable labor and gunplay, cleaned out Excelsior. Briar and his crew were imprisoned, and that was the last Fargo had heard of him till tonight, when Modoc indicated his father was out free.

It made a man wonder who was leading the outlaws now . . .

Fargo did not go to his room. He stopped at the door to Wild Rose Burleigh's room, tapping softly. When she asked, he gave his name, and a moment later a sleepy-eyed Rose opened the door.

"My room was searched, really tossed," Fargo explained. "I just as soon not trust to sleep in there tonight, especially with the mattress torn up."

Rose smiled languidly, ushering him in. "I get it. You came to me looking for a hole for the night . . ."

That was putting it mildly, Fargo soon realized; he'd boxed himself in a hole, down at the deep end, and was having a hard time. For whenever he insisted he had to get up early and craved some shut-eye, Rose would obligingly get him up. Somehow she always managed to touch a soft spot and provoke a rise out of him, persisting till it grew out of hand and they had to get it straight between them again . . . and over again . . . while Fargo tried gamely to stick firm, aware he was sinking if not already sunk, and braced to go down at his post . . .

The cold morning had a gunmetal gray overcast that hung in the air, as though the weather was pondering whether to storm or not. Fargo was out in it at first light, intent on tracing down Chilton's pack as soon as possible, hopefully before the express was divided up and scattered by the thieves. He combed the area around and adjacent to Puckett's Palace, then rousted Thorne at the stable, collected his horse, and rode out on a quick survey of high spots.

Nothing came of that. Fargo was soon back at the trading post, the light marginally better but still not strong enough for him to traipse along the river. For a time he perused the street in front of the post, looking for tracks. Not surprisingly, he found plenty. It also seemed to intrigue rubberneckers, and as more of Lewiston got up and about, a motley bunch gathered and milled about, asking questions, offering advice, and getting in Fargo's way.

Shortly the group was joined by a man Fargo recognized from yesterday's poker session—the card-playing blacksmith, Vern Koehler. Unshaved and slightly drunk, Koehler watched awhile, then motioned Fargo aside.

"There's your clue," he declared, pointing to a hoofprint. "Right there. He hitched his horse near the door, blowed the safe, rode to the river, and gave the loot to his partners. I'm a smithy, I know. I can glance at a horseshoe imprint and if I see it again inside a week or two, I'll remember it. Find the horse that made this print, and we've got a lead to our man. If you've a mind to, I'll help you look at every hoof in town and—"

Koehler choked off, staring at the print Fargo's horse had just left in the snow as it fidgeted at the hitchrail. Abruptly Koehler started to retreat. "Forget I said a word, pal. I'm forgetting all I know about hoofprints. I know when I'm well off."

"Hold on," Fargo said, frowning. "What's with you?"

"I just noticed," Koehler said uneasily, "your horse's fresh hoofprint. Then I looked at the one left by the robber's horse— just to make sure. It's the same. Your horse was used in last night's robbery." He backed away. "Now, get this straight. I ain't saying you'd anything to do with it. I ain't saying nothing here, I'm shoving off right quick for Excelsior."

Fargo's annoyance increased. By now everybody around must be aware that no one except himself and maybe Thorne could've handled his ornery horse. Thorne's family background must be known by others, too. Already Fargo could detect suspicious glances being exchanged between those who were looking on. If need be, he could drag in Wild Rose to alibi his whereabouts, he supposed, but short of that he'd get nowhere arguing and would be better off sidestepping it.

"What's up in Excelsior?" Fargo asked the blacksmith.

"I live there. Ran out of tobacco and horseshoe nails," Koehler answered. "Came down for what I needed, and to get any mail."

"Ride?"

"Naw. Snow's too deep. A horse can get through okay, but it can't pack no lead. More trouble than they're worth this time of year." With that, Koehler nodded with a grim, tight-lipped expression and stalked away.

Fargo spent most of the day scouting the banks of Snake River for the sign he needed so badly. He found Modoc Thorne's canoe shattered in a log jam. And two miles beyond he located the robbers' boat in a similar jam. A rip near the stern proved his bullet had entered at that point, and gone out the opposite side close to the waterline.

There was a possibility the men had been drowned and the express pack was on the riverbed. Fargo reconnoitered the bank above and below, but found nothing except hoofmarks where a wild horse had evidently come to drink. No bodies, no prints. Stymied, he regarded the mountainous horizon with frustration, wondering where to continue, what to try now.

A whisper of a thought. Fargo strained to catch it, but the impression faded silently away. He focused on the more salient point, buttressed by the blacksmith's jawboner this morning, that the thief had used his Ovaro. Who else could control the animal besides Thorne? It fit together—like father, like son, on a job like the ambusher would pull. It fit to order—no one else could be accused of it, while Thorne couldn't get out of it. Everything wrapped in one neat package.

Trouble was, it fit too tidily in one piece, too pat to suit Fargo. Not that he'd put it past Thorne or forget his own suspicions. But Thorne didn't strike him as the only crook in these parts, a single hellion raiding trails, safes, Amity, and running the livery. Also, if he'd the smarts and made the loot, surely Thorne wouldn't be a hostler camping in a feed room. Besides, Thorne couldn't be so dumb he'd rustle his own stable and steal, for whatever reason or fluke, the one horse that'd hang him.

Another tack had to be taken, and the impression of that first thought returned, haunting Fargo by its very elusiveness. It refused to form, obstinately pale. It was a nothing, and yet . . .

Checking his horse and the gear and tightening cinch straps, Fargo started back to Lewiston. Nigh on mid-afternoon, he judged, though the dull gray day had remained unaltered since morning, the shrouded overcast hovering without any breaks, without any signals of the weather ahead. It could change suddenly at any time, and to what was anyone's guess. Again Fargo scanned the rise of near foothills, mindful of the weather while gazing northeastward, sweeping higher along snow-buried vastnesses of brush and timber, sheer ravines and craggy steeps of desolation— northeastward across unseen passes, where far beyond view lay the mountain valley of Excelsior.

From scuttlebutt Fargo had heard, the trail to Excelsior took from dawn to dusk. Maybe that was on short winter days, probably not, but certainly he'd never reach Excelsior today. He'd have to pitch camp, in uncertain if not downright perverse weather. It made sense to stay the night and set off in the morning, when he could see how the weather was shaping up.

Tough. As soon as he stocked up supplies, he'd head out. Generally he listened to reason, especially his own, yet he couldn't fully explain why he wasn't this time. What failed to come through logically, though, succeeded intuitively. He'd found his gut instinct reliable, and now, as through a glass darkly, Fargo sensed what to do, where to go.

To find wolves, find a wolf's den.

Excelsior had cropped up twice now, not directly tied to the theft but in related ways. Enough to call it to mind. Tough country up there, in the best times of year. Home to renegade half-breeds and bleach-eyed owlhoots, who made it clear to strangers that they were unwelcome in Excelsior. Bandit Briar Thorne had made his home and his stand there, and for all Fargo knew, the old reprobate could be back in stock and trade. And Vern Koehler lived up there. The blacksmith might not want to talk to him, or if he did, Fargo wasn't sure he would help. Still, the idea persisted, gradually solidifying as he rode into town.

Fargo road up to Hi Pockets' trading post, the remains of which its owner and a party of helpers had managed to put back in order. An interested group gathered around Fargo as he filled his saddlebags with trail grub.

"You know as much as I do," Fargo responded when asked the latest news. "I only know that much from Hi Pockets, and I'm inclined to agree that it's the botched work of a few scummy, cutthroat morons. First, they didn't time their raid right. He's told y'all how his safe is usually flush, but just then held odds'n ends, nothing worth more than my pack. I found their canoe in a log jam. It had smashed while moving fast with a heavy load."

The significance of this information wasn't lost on a group of men who used canoes a lot. "Bodies still in the river—maybe," one man muttered, and a second suggested, "Might find the swag next summer when the water's low." Another drawled, "It ain't liable to float away, what's in that bag," and the others laughed.

"You never can tell," Fargo said as he remounted. "I'm keeping my eyes open, for one. They might've left the river where I ain't checked yet."

Leaving them to infer that was his destination, Fargo pulled out and never looked back.

The elevation of Lewiston was a few hundred feet. Diablo Pass was nine thousand feet, traversed by a poor excuse of a wagon road open in the summer and a trail in the winter, often over snow packed so hard that it was ice. Frequently there would be a stretch of several weeks when snowstorms made it impossible for anything to cross. Other times, just the accumulation of snow would block the pass.

The trail was typical of mountain routes, tending to follow the meanderings of swiftly flowing creeks. For a while at first, Fargo had been able to maintain a steady pace that covered the early miles without overtaxing his horse. That tapered off as the trail kept climbing, steepening. By the time the sky hinted dimly of dusk, Fargo was well on his ascent into deepening snows.

Fargo made no attempt to ride. The Ovaro would manage to flounder through the drifts at this high altitude and take him along if he insisted, but that was too much of a burden for any horse a man respected. As he neared the summit, progress grew slower. He breathed faster, deeper, to draw as much air into his lungs as possible. The pinto's breathing was audible, heart beating violently against its ribs.

A cold blast of air moaned steadily through the pass. There was a crust on the snow, and a thousand feet below, clouds rushed through the air and broke as the ragged peaks shredded them. Fargo pushed onward, wary of the overcast while absorbing the grandeur of the scene, until abruptly his eyes caught something foreign to the natural beauty—a splash of crimson on the snow.

In the vast, even expanse of pure white, the red patch stood out like a fresh blaze on a tree. Fargo stared intently at the irregular spot. It was blood, alright, blood that had frozen almost as soon as it touched the snow. He removed the crust in the immediate vicinity and cautiously brushed away the layers of snow. Each layer was different. There had been a wet snow, then powder, and after that a hailstorm, then another wet snow. A passing animal or man had smashed through the layers and packed down the snow.

"A boot, and a helluva big boot," Fargo muttered as he identified a human foot print, and immediately thought of the blacksmith. "Yeah, here's a print he left going. And here's a later one, left on his return. He went out light and returned carrying a pack. Horseshoe nails, grub, and mail, seems it was."

A few minutes later he found a hoofprint. "Wild horse," he concluded, "or at least an unshod horse. No indication that it was shod." Kicking the snow back into place, he stirred his Ovaro into action. "We're almost to the top," he said encouragingly. "Another twenty minutes and we'll have a downhill haul."

They crested the pass in fifteen. Descending the far side, Fargo studied the sky with added concern. The waning day now dwindled in twilight, verging on nightfall, and he'd yet to spot a likely campsite. On this side of the summit ridgeline, the low overcast was swirling, buffeted by some upper-air turbulence, such as a weather front speeding from the east. The overcast was shoved on ahead and smashed against the mountain rims, scattering like dirty gray whirls of buckshot.

On the crest of a ridge studded with windblown, ravaged scrub, Fargo stopped, abruptly aware that the wind had suddenly shifted and with it came a piercing cold. He eyed the splintered, low-hanging cloud cover and he knew what this meant. A blizzard. The kind that swept down with fierce suddenness out of the northeast, bending trees before its cannonade of snow and hurricane winds.

For a quarter of a mile he forced himself and the Ovaro to keep moving. The dying rays of twilight were retreating steadily until luminance lingered only on the broad, bare stretches of reflective snow. But by then Fargo had found his campsite. A sheltered spot, blackened stones and stumps marked it as a favorite site. The wind grew in pitch and volume as he set up camp, and it was a contest of strength and will to set up the canvas shelter flap and weigh it down with heavy chunks from a nearby deadfall.

Finally hunching by the fire, Fargo cooked up a quick dinner and coffee. A new gust of wind, heavier and damper then before, brought the smell of snow riding with it. Then the first few flakes began to fall, whispering down in gentle eddies to disappear in the licking flames. Sometime soon tonight the snow would come—white blinding snow so thick a man could hardly see a hand before his face.

On that cheery thought, Fargo bedded down for the night. He was tired with the tiredness of lusty health, and dropped off to sleep almost immediately . . .

Sometime later he awoke to find two dim, parka-swathed figures bending over him. He started to heave up. A long revolver barrel rapped against his forehead, and he slumped back, gritting his teeth. His brain spun crazily and his muscles seemed suddenly sapped of strength.

Vaguely he sensed that rough, strong hands were half-dragging, half-carrying him from the tent. Blasting cold wind helped revive his dazed senses, and he was able to focus on the men as he was hauled on his feet.

He might've guessed.

Damrow and Trent.

9

Damrow had his parka hood drawn close about his face, concealing his features, but Skye Fargo would've recognized the big-nosed, gourd-shaped slob anywhere. In turn, Damrow watched Fargo with his revolver following every move. Mostly Fargo watched for a break, a careless moment as Trent took his rifle and searched out his revolver in his mackinaw.

Damrow aimed his revolver dead-center at Fargo's gut. "Where's that ring?"

"Find it," Fargo said.

"Sure."

Damrow, bending his head so that Fargo could not catch a glimpse of his face, began a quick, systematic search. He gave a satisfied grunt, stepped back and pocketed the fake diamond ring Joel Dumas had lost to Fargo. Turning to Trent then, Damrow said, "Orders is, orders does. Let's move. We took too damn long playing tag with this prick as it was. Meet you in Excelsior."

The wind was reaching gale proportions, forcing Damrow to repeat himself. Trying to catch the words, Fargo was glancing around the camp, taking in every detail as the cold bit through his clothing and gnawed into his marrow. Trent made no effort to obey, and Damrow got furious.

"What's holding you up?" he shouted over the moaning into the trees.

"Can't make it noplace this storm. We sit tight until it stops."

"No, we don't, Trent," Damrow snapped. "You get them nags facin' right and start toward Excelsior."

But the weather had plans of its own. The steel gray wall that Fargo had seen advancing since the wind changed suddenly engulfed them. In a howling fury the blizzard was upon them, hurtling half frozen snow in a horizontal path, snatching the canvas shelter like a dead leaf and whipping it away, hurtling Trent prostrate as it struck him and covered the campsite with a blinding sheet of grayness.

For an instant Damrow was distracted while he glanced over at Trent. In that instant Fargo stepped forward and punched a stiffened knuckle-duster smack into Damrow's Adam's apple, while making a grab for the pistol with his other hand. But he missed the pistol, Damrow reacting extremely fast by lurching backward, gagging, tears springing to his eyes. In a strange, rubbery wilting, he collapsed to the ground, left hand clawing at the throat, choking raggedly, trying to suck in air. With his right hand he was still trying to train his revolver at Fargo.

Fargo dove to his hands and knees, crawling toward the spot where he had seen Trent prop his rifle. Moving from memory alone, his eyes useless in the white hell, he groped his way around the ashpit of his long cold campfire. Unseeing, he bumped into another form.

He swung at the man with his fist, saw that it was Trent. He missed as the roaring wind caused him to lose his balance while Trent brought up his rifle, sighting it. For an agonizing second, Fargo struggled for his balance, found it, and lunged to one side.

Red flame licked out at him, the roar of the gun lost in the greater sound of the storm. Dimly Fargo heard the cussing bellow of Damrow coming his way, and, veering, he launched into the blizzard. Lead snarled around his ears as Trent and Damrow loosened salvos from their weapons. Tearing on through the concealing snow torrent, Fargo was quickly past the point of just wasting bullets, though he added a short margin of error and then came to a halt.

Nobody shot again, but he knew they knew his direction.

Fargo stood for a moment, recalling the terrain he had scrutinized for campsites before the storm. Then, with his head down against the bitter blast, he moved slowly toward a remembered ridge and its sparse growth of stunted spruce. The curving slope of the hill rang a chime in him, and gladly he followed it, groping for a firm footing. For an hour he went on, keeping his left leg on higher ground than his right until he was sure he was far enough away to be safe when the storm abated.

Dizzy from fatigue, he could not catch himself when one foot met empty air. Down he went into a black nothingness that seemed to go on forever. Then a shocking impact that sent light spinning through his head. Unfeeling, he lay awhile. Reason, numbed with cold, was as helpless as his flaccid body. But the flame flickered still. Get up, idiot. Move. Stamp your feet. Or lie here and die like a hound.

It took all his will and all his ebbing strength to

rise on one elbow. He dragged himself toward the wall of rock where he had fallen down. He climbed somehow to his haunches, squatting there against the cold rock, shielded from the piercing lances of the wind.

And then, in the way of the Northwest, the blizzard began to lose force. The moan of the winds had died to a whisper. Fargo saw, less than five yards away, a thicket of dead twigs and branches piled up against a stunted shrub. He had to light a match with his teeth to set the twigs alight. Then fire, and blessed warmth, and the awful pain of flesh—cold flesh—coming back to life.

Huddled close to the fire's warmth, Fargo flayed himself for letting them catch him unawares. Well, there'd be hell to pay yet. Half lost high on the shank of back beyond, no supplies, no horse, no weapons aside from his knife. He brooded, snarling sulfurous curses to keep himself awake.

In the shadowy darkness of early morning, Fargo roused and began stamping the circulation back into his stiffened limbs. Then he set off on a long hike.

Later, with the graying of dawn, Fargo watched from behind a rock outcropping as Damrow and Trent broke camp. He saw his Ovaro loaded like a packhorse, then roped behind Damrow's mount as they started off for Excelsior.

Stumbling in the frequent drifts, he followed the ridges eastward. The horses would be slow, encumbered by riders, trailblazing through the powdery new snow. On grades and through hollows they could make little time. A man on foot could do just as well cutting overland and concealing himself in the flats below.

Finally Fargo found a spot he liked and settled

down to await their coming in the shelter of a steeply undercut bank.

He heard Damrow first, cussing belligerently as he forced his horse through the snow. Then Damrow and Fargo's pinto came into view, but Trent was no where to be seen. Fargo smiled in satisfaction. They were afraid of him. Trent was probably riding parallel, concealed in the shelter of the trees, waiting for Fargo to give himself away. Damrow was too far out in the open to get at, even to shoot at accurately— if Fargo had had a rifle to shoot with.

Fargo had timed it well, though. Damrow had not yet passed from sight when he reined up and Trent appeared out of the trees across the way. They pitched camp and one tended the fire while the other stood guard outside the circle of light.

With the pangs of hunger gnawing at his vitals, Fargo cursed them as he crossed the open space far back and made his way forward until he picked up the end of Trent's trail. There he waited up in the deep niche of a large frost-split boulder until Trent came back to take up the trail again. Peering between its sharply divided sections, Fargo had a good perspective of the area immediately around him.

Pretty soon, in the sharply outlined section within his view, Trent appeared on horseback. Gripping his knife tightly, Fargo slid the ball of his left thumb over its blade and waited.

Trent was riding slowly between the rocks and trees, rifle clasped tightly as he checked right and left. He looked right when he should have looked left because Fargo was there, leaping at him from the rock niche. Gawking, Trent jerked spasmodically, wrenching loose of his saddle as Fargo barreled into him and carried him tumbling to the ground. Scrambling upright, Fargo made a jabbing gesture toward Trent's eyes to shock him, to intimidate him into surrender.

"Drop the gun." Fargo ordered. "Don't move."

Trent slipped on the icy ground, and out of sheer luck and desperation managed to parry Fargo's thrust with his rifle. Fargo missed his face but not by much. He could actually see Trent pale with fear, even as Trent recovered and aimed at him.

"She-it! I'll blow your head off for this!"

Trent was fast, but not fast enough. Already Fargo was dropping to one knee, his other leg outstretched, in a countering move that brought him inside the arc of the swiveling rifle. Springing up, he clamped the deflected barrel with his left hand and yanked it toward him, which bringing the knife ripping across Trent's front. The blade tore open the parka at the neckline and made a slender gash diagonally from breastbone to ribs before slicing through the thick muscles of Trent's forearm. The wounded man wavered, his rifle falling from nerveless fingers.

"No more trouble," Fargo stated. "You understand?"

Stunned, Trent stared with bulging eyes. Something about his stare stopped Fargo cold, for he had seen that expression before a time or two. It was the look of a man facing death. The next instant, Fargo knew why. Trent reached toward his throat, and just before his fingers covered his neck, Fargo saw a flap of skin fall away and a spitting cloud of blood erupt. He had reacted defensively, hastily, his knife thrust not only cutting Trent's chest and arm but inadvertently slashing his throat before that.

Trent tried to stem the tidal wave of crimson with his fingers, but it didn't work. The liquid oozed around his hands, turning his front into a sodden scarlet mess in seconds. As Fargo watched, he fell back, seemingly in slow motion, and crumpled to the ground.

Fargo turned away. "Hell."

Damrow was making poor time. Fargo came even with him in less than a mile. Some while later, Fargo dismounted from Trent's horse and crouched along the trees as Damrow stopped to build a fire and cook some food. Saliva running in his mouth, he forced himself to steadiness, taking careful aim with Trent's rifle. But the range was still too far and a cross-breeze had picked up. Disgusted, he fired in hopes of coming close enough to scare Damrow into hiding.

An answering shot whistled wide of the mark and Fargo grinned. Damrow yelled in anger toward the woods, "Hey, Trent. Where the hell you gone?" Then, apparently suspecting the truth, he stopped.

Until the light faded, Fargo kept Damrow pinned down. Then, in the cloaking darkness, he edged toward the cookfire. Crawling through the snow from hummock to hummock, he drew near enough finally to see the dim form of Damrow. A little more and he could get the drop on him. He inched his way, praying that the horses would not react to him.

A brittle limb hidden under the snow cracked beneath Fargo's gliding weight. He swore under his breath as his horse looked up. Quiet, he pleaded. But it was Damrow's mount that let out a nervous whinny. In a flash Damrow leaped up, saw Fargo, and snapped a hasty shot. Fargo, shouldering the rifle, fired at Damrow. They both missed. Fargo saw the blackness of a jutting rock nearby and edged over to it for shelter. Damrow, left without cover, retreated hastily to the bordering woods.

Swiveling, Fargo almost triggered a quick snap-shot at Damrow. But Damrow was zigzagging in the darkness, a poor target to begin with, and Fargo knew from having counted his loads that he had chambered his final shot. For a moment he huddled there motionless, depressed, until the terrible pangs of hunger drove all else from his mind.

He crawled to the campfire and tore like an animal into the food Damrow had prepared. Every scrap was gone before the awful pain in his belly eased. He fought against sleep, his eyes probing the shadows. Things seemed to move, blurred shapes, but then they grew still again.

Fargo started toward the Ovaro, figuring the pack it was lugging would most likely carry his revolver or rifle—only to suddenly halt, catching his breath at the sound abruptly filling the silence. Dimly, through peering eyes, he glimpsed a shadow detach itself from the line of trees. Damrow—bolder now because of a greater fear. A flash of red flame split the night, a bullet thudding into the pack on the pinto.

When no answering shot came, Damrow edged closer. Now and then the man crouched nervously, looking back over his shoulder at the forest, fearful of ending up stranded in the open. Fatigue was making Fargo drowsy in spite of his tenseness. Now he could hear the crunch of boot steps in the snow. Then a triumphant laugh.

"By hell!" Damrow gloated as he charged, taking aim. "Caught you empty-gunned! You're shot!"

Those were the last words Damrow ever spoke on earth. From point-blank range Trent's rifle erupted, spewing fire into the darkness, drilling a slug into Damrow's fat gut and shattering his spine between his kidneys. Damrow twisted and pitched forward, and for a few seconds before death claimed him the pain must have been horrific, because his agonized screams came through the roar of gunfire.

Straightening, Fargo stared at Damrow through the haze of gunpowder smoke until confident the man was dead, not feining. Then he went and collected enough dry wood to stoke a blazing fire, unpacked his Ovaro, and found his weapons. Later he piled snow into a crude mound. It would have to suffice for a grave, just as a similar mound had for Trent.

10

Less than two hours later, Skye Fargo reached the straggling group of canvas, sod, and log structures called Excelsior. Despite the hour—or maybe due to it—residents seemed ready and raring, lamplight filtering through numerous tents and dirt-rimed windowpanes.

Riding in, Fargo caught the odor of coal smoke issuing from the blacksmith shop and soon he heard the ring of hammer against anvil. Vern Koehler, in a seared leather apron, came out of his shop and cast him a leery eye.

"Fargo? What're you doing here?"

"Looking for loot."

"Well, don't look at me just 'cause I looked at your horse," Koehler said resentfully, "or 'cause I live in Excelsior. This ain't no outlaw haven no more, but a law-abiding community."

"Naturally. I'm not here just because of a bad reputation," Fargo hedged.

"Y'mean, you really got onto something?"

"I got a hunch you might know, maybe. Being a smithy and traipsing around some, you'd get to know the latest goings-on, all the curious tidbits that I wouldn't catch."

"If I was so privy, why would I tell you?"

"You're law-abiding, naturally."

"That's kind of crowding me, pal. There was a time when you'd been told off with long guns and pistols, but nobody now yearns for confrontations. And luckily I'm an agreeable sort." Koehler didn't sound too agreeable, and his coal-blackened face showed not merely resentment but temper. "So happens maybe I've a guess what brung you. Trapper name of Mooch Paulson showed up late last night, I gather, and for once he didn't cadge a drink. He was flush and buyin' rounds for everybody—with gold dust. The beggar's never had a poke before."

Fargo rubbed his earlobe. "Where'd this Paulson go from here?"

"That I don't know." Koehler broke into a grin that somehow didn't match his cranky stolidness. "He mightn't have left. When he's blind soused, Mooch sometimes bunks over with one of the guys. Tell you what, Fargo, you go put up at Zerbe's store, and I'll see if I can't ferret out a little more."

"Thanks," Fargo said. He rode on slowly down the street.

A sullen fourteen-year-old boy appeared as Fargo dismounted in front of Zerbe's store. 'I'll take your nag," he said.

"You'll take all three," Fargo responded, motioning to Damrow's and Trent's horses strung behind his Ovaro. "You'll tend to them proper, too."

The boy pocketed the dollar Fargo gave him. "Nice pinto." Like most Excelsior males, he knew a good horse when he saw one. "Well, there's the barn. If you ask polite, Ma might dish you up some leftover chow."

Zerbe's store was a long, rambling structure, with a potbelly stove in the center of the room. The benches were greasy and notched where men had idly carved as they talked. Shelves groaned under the burden of trade goods, and there was the blended smell of rope, paint, cheese, spice, and whale oil in the air. Zerbe, round-shouldered and harried, was constantly on the run. Fargo recalled hearing old lawdogs reminisce that with the exception of Briar Thorne, Zerbe's father had covered more territory than any outlaw in Excelsior—and never left his store.

"Hello," Zerbe greeted, "upstairs, first cubby on left is yours, fifty cents a night, meals two bits." He hurried on.

Fargo dumped his warbag and returned to the main room, where Zerbe's stout wife served him a hefty bowl of steaming gallimaufry stew. From time to time men stopped in for supplies or to lounge awhile, talking among themselves, neither friendly nor hostile toward Fargo, but simply ignoring him. He took no offense. They were a hard, wary bunch, descended from Briar Thorne's bandit gang, he assumed, and even if they were now as law-abiding as Koehler would have him believe, they would by temperament and experience be prone to shun strangers.

Faintly, from farther down the street, could be heard a piano banging and a violin screeching an accompaniment above the unmistakable raucous noise of a saloon in full snort. About the time Fargo finished his stew and was thinking to head that way, he heard the crash of glass, a gunshot, then the swift hoofbeat of a burdened horse in flight.

"Somebody jumped through a winder," Zerbe remarked.

Nobody thought enough of that to bother responding. Fargo walked across to the door and met two men hastening in from the street—bearded brutes smelling of dried fish and raw pelts.

Zerbe asked, "What happened? Somebody jump through a winder?"

"Nothing happened," one of the bearded duo said, shaking his head with an air of a man who couldn't get over it. "Mooch lurches in shouldering saddlebags, pulls his poke out of 'em, slaps it on the bar and says, 'Drinks for everybody. Set 'em up.' Drunker'n seven barflies at a barbecue. He gets his red-eye and downs it and the saddlebags slips off and falls clunk on the floor. Right next to Gil McHenry. 'Sound heavy,' McHenry said friendly-like. 'You carryin' rock?' He laughs a big hearty laugh. 'Podner,' Mooch hollers, 'that ain't nothin' but money. I earned it,' he says, 'an' I got it. I pulled it over on 'em,' he says, 'and I aim to step high and wide and handsome now on. To heel with 'em,' he says, 'I was smart enough to get it and I'm smart enough to keep it. If anyone dreams he's man enough to get it away from me, let him step right up where you is, including you!"

"And?" Zerbe urged impatiently.

"And Mooch knifed Gil McHenry," the other bearded man answered. "Then he walked through the window, swung a saddle, and lit shuck."

"Jes-sus! McHenry hurt much?"

"Don't know, Zerbe. Vern Koehler took him home."

One of the other men suggested, "Mooch's headed over the pass?"

"Naw, back country. He's got them shanties along his trap line," one bearded man replied. The other nodded agreement and added, "He'll be a hard bugger to find."

There was more of it, but that was enough for Fargo. He scented blood.

As Excelsior drowsed under murky dawn skies, Fargo saddled his horse and took after Mooch Paulson. Having stayed up last night until the others had run dry of talk, he had pieced a fairly clear picture of what and where to hunt. Still, Paulson held all the advantages. The fugitive had a night's head start, knew the country, and could double back on his trail or leave no trail at all, and any kind of wind flurry would sweep his tracks out of existence. While Fargo had to dismount repeatedly to check up, those tracks were all he had to chart a course across the frozen white reaches.

Shortly before noon he rode into a fenced clearing where a tired horse viewed his arrival without interest. Fargo checked the hoofprints and saw that this was Mooch Paulson's horse. Working swiftly, he fashioned loops that would hold his pack and his rolled-up furs on his shoulder. He left the Ovaro in the corral to feed and rest, and set out on foot to track down his man.

The trail, faint most of the time, led up a gouge in the mountainside, down which a small stream tumbled. Often Fargo had to use his hands to pull himself up the slope. He gained a ridge and found Paulson's tracks leading in the direction of a network of peaks and crevices. He knew he must be crowding Paulson, and he forced himself onward until his lungs were sobbing for air and his heart threatened to pound a hole through his ribs.

Looking back, Fargo could barely make out Excelsior far below. Diablo Pass towered against a lackluster sky, but instead of being gleaming white and sharply defined, the notch was streaked with brown. In the distance it looked as if someone had carelessly dropped a piece of brown shoelace on the snow.

As Fargo watched, the brown area shifted downward, leaving the pass white again. Suddenly he understood. A band of wild horses was coming through the pass to Excelsior valley. That was fortunate, he thought, for the band would pack down the trail and make his return ride easier.

Paulson's trail curved off through the stunted brush to the north. Fargo pursued remorselessly, the steady crunch of his boot steps in the frozen snow like a drumbeaten march. And he was gaining. Signs indicated that he had cut Mooch Paulson's lead by half. Then in late afternoon a breeze arose. By dusk it had become a biting wind down from the northeast, scudding the snow and blurring tracks.

With growing difficulty Fargo made out the trail through a fringed underbrush. He came out the other side onto the smooth ice of a lake, where the knifelike wind was blowing elfish snow devils across the surface. Surely Paulson had crossed sometime earlier in the day. Nary a trace of his route remained, and no telling in the snow-swirling wind and gathering dark how large the lake or at what point Paulson had left it. Nothing to do but wait for morning yet again.

"But the skunk'll have to hole up, too," Fargo reasoned. Finding shelter in a deeply undercut bank, he kindled a fire and ate, huddling in his furs and nursing his own meager warmth. "Paulson can't be far ahead. And if he stayed within this area, I should connect farther on."

Nor was Fargo wrong. The situation was disheartening at dawn, Paulson's trail totally obliterated on the freshly scoured expanse. But Fargo patiently studied the opposite shore a mile away while he heated food and coffee. Straight ahead was a valley that led out through some moundlike knolls. To the left rose slopes looking rougher than a cob, while eastward the country ran off into heavy timber and chasms. Paulson couldn't have been far beyond the lake when the wind struck. A direct advance to his location should leave their relative positions unchanged.

"I'm betting on that valley," Fargo decided aloud. "It's most probable, the way he was heading."

Late morning brought Fargo to an abandoned campsite. A gleam shone in his eyes as he surveyed the trampled snow, picking up Paulson's trail and forging on grimly. Toward evening he took a breather, relaxing by a rock rim, tired and anxious to end the pursuit but not caring to risk being caught amid the crevasses after dark. The wind had died before morning, but now a vagrant breeze carried the odor of woodsmoke. Fargo, looking to his left, saw a column of smoke rising from a shoulder not far ahead.

As the breeze died down, the smoke column lifted high above the peaks. Mooch Paulson, the great trapper and mountain man, was burning green wood. "The damn fool," Fargo growled. "He must think nobody could've followed him, either too soft to keep up the chase or turned back. Only a fool builds a fire when he's on the lam, and I'd like to bet this is the first time an Excelsior man has been guilty of that dumb trick."

He reviewed the difficulties encountered thus far in hunting Mooch Paulson. Repeatedly he had found himself admiring the skill with which Paulson had thrown him off the scent. Paulson was nobody's fool. "There's a bare chance I'm the damned fool," he growled to himself as it dawned on him that Paulson seemed to make pursuit awful easy at times. Too easy. The more Fargo thought of it, the more he was inclined to believe Paulson was drawing on the chase, and if so, then it meant the fight in Excelsior had been staged to get him out of the way.

He dropped down to the nearest timber, built a fire, and got a little rest. He hoped Paulson, and anyone from Excelsior who might be dogging him, would see the glare of his fire and conclude he had camped for the night.

Three hours' rest worked wonders. He retraced his path back to the lake, caught a few hours of shut-eye in the same undercut shelter, and next morning headed back to the corral. There he saddled his pinto and headed for Excelsior. The settlement was splattered with lanternlight when he reached its outskirts after nightfall.

At Zerbe's store a lamp was aglow in only one of the second floor rooms. The light flashed on and off at regular intervals, as though someone were signaling. Fargo sat asaddle for several minutes, focusing on the window and trying to decipher a code from the blinking light. Still puzzled, he jiggered his horse toward it, and, approaching, he glimpsed someone pacing the floor and passing repeatedly in front of the lamp. This was no signal, but the nervous actions of a person too troubled to sleep. His horse continued sidling closer until Fargo stiffened, startled to see that the pacer was Amity Dumas.

Muttering under his breath, Fargo tied his horse to a clump of brush, kept to the shadows, and cautiously approached the building. Zerbe and his family were either asleep or watching for his return. The latter appeared unlikely because he had arranged pretty convincing evidence he was still on Mooch Paulson's trail. He gathered up several pebbles and tossed them at the window.

Amity ceased pacing and blew out the lamp. When nothing more happened, Fargo threw some more pebbles while calling her name in a whisper. The window opened and she leaned out, hissing down, "That you, Skye?"

"Yeah, now, why're you here?"

"My dust was stolen, the whole trunk."

Fargo sighed. "Sorry. But it was a sitting duck in your room."

"It was in the hotel safe. I took your advice and left it there."

"Christ. Hang on, I'll fetch a ladder so we can talk," Fargo responded hastily. "I'm starting to savvy a lot of things."

Moments later Fargo returned with a ladder from the barn. Placing it against the building, he climbed stealthily to Amity's window, on over the sill, and quietly to the floor. She was close alongside, breathing anxiously, one hand toward her heart, her wide lambent eyes centered on him.

"How was the hotel safe hit?" Fargo asked. "Blown like Hi Pocket's?"

Amity nodded. "Very late, nobody about, except for the lady who dozes there, Miss Bottomly, and she was knocked out before she knew it. They escaped with a big haul this time, more than I'd of guessed, but it turns out plenty of folks were storing valuables, bullion, you name it, in the safe, confidentially, like a private vault. And then . . . then

124

some men got drunk at Puckett's and took it upon themselves to arrest Modoc for the robbery. They were holding him and wondering who'd go bring the law, a—and I imagine they won't do worse to him, maybe even sober up and realize how silly they've been."

Fargo could see the dejected slump of her shoulders, the quaver in her voice. But he made no mistaken move to offer sympathy, a comforting shoulder, aware of her feisty independence from before and needing no new wrangles now. Instead he struck a match and stepped to the lamp, relighting it very low. When he looked around, she had regained her spirit and composure.

"Tell me about Modoc," Fargo said.

"Modoc went to play cards with Old Bill Reed, and I hadn't seen him all evening. I wouldn't have known where'd he gone, and normally don't, except he chanced to mention it earlier in passing. Next thing I know, I'm flung out of bed by the safe exploding. Everybody comes running and looking then, except I don't see Modoc. Later these drunk men come knocking on the door, demanding to know where Modoc is. Well, I told them in no uncertain terms they'd never find a man in my place at any such time of night. That's when Modoc happened to wander in the hotel, curious about the safe blowing, and they nabbed him. I explained he had been playing cards with Old Bill Reed, but Modoc admitted Bill wasn't home when he got there," the girl concluded dejectedly.

"Then what did you do?" Fargo asked.

Amity was staring at him with fascination, the way she might have stared at a wildcat. She seemed to shake herself, then she answered, "I searched around the lobby for clues, but didn't find a thing. Too many people had tracked up the floor maybe, and as soon as it was daylight I decided to ride up here and find you."

"How'd you know I was here?"

"Why, Hi Pockets told me, I believe."

"Uh-huh. What was the trail like?"

"Well packed," the girl answered. "A band of wild horses had been over it. They'd come over the pass and were grazing along the snow line. They came back late afternoon a couple of days ago."

"You go back to bed and get some rest," Fargo suggested. "I got some moseying to do, I think."

Amity made no move, no gesture to indicate she wanted to. She was watching him in a very strange way, almost a shameless stare. When she made no response to his suggestion, Fargo gave her a new appraisal; a knotted muscle rippled up his cheekbone as he said gently, "Yes, I better go now."

"If you must." She still did not move, but stayed close to him, her eyes gripping his. He felt the force of a sudden chemistry between them, and knew that she wanted his kiss. There was no mistaking that. A part of him resisted, but it was lost in the throbbing as he slipped his hand around behind her and drew her forward. Her eyes widened, her breathing quickened, and for a moment she pushed her palms against his chest, drawing back. But her lips parted slowly and the thrust of her hands relaxed; her arms went around him and there was sudden urgency in her hungry kiss.

When they broke, Amity murmured, "I'll close the curtain." She went to the window, pulling the curtains together and without pausing began to take off her clothes. She was wearing a man's range garb and it didn't take long for her to strip naked. Fargo's clothes were heaped on the floor almost as fast, and they stood gazing at each other naked, smiling, before moving to the narrow cot of a bed, where they lay down together in a heated embrace.

Fargo had traveled similar exotic routes with independent women, and, true to type, Amity did not care for coyness or prolonged buildups. Hers was an elemental need, and once she had made up her mind, she pursued her target with a minimum of ruffles and flourishes. At times Fargo preferred the no-nonsense approach—such as now, when, having gone through that long track cross-country, he had little energy left and less desire for appetizers or spectacular productions.

He cupped her breasts and sucked one of her nipples. She acted as though she expected him to bite it, but in a moment she was stroking his hair and pushing him closer, and Fargo knew she liked the sensation of it. He suckled on both her breasts until, wriggling, she crushed herself along his body, wrapping one leg over him . . . and then she hesitated, drawing in her breath, waiting for him to accept or reject. With an inward smile, he turned over on his back. Amity then raised herself and squatted astride his pelvis with her knees on either side of his hips. There, gazing down at him with passion, she rose and impaled herself on his spear, contracting her strong thighs so that the muscular action clamped her passage tightly around his rigid manhood.

Fargo clenched his buttocks, thrusting his hips off the bed. Amity spread her thighs so that, sliding up and down, she soon contained the whole of his shaft in her squeezing loins. Her head sagged forward, then was flung back. Fargo grasped her jiggling breasts, toying with them until she bent to kiss him. Then again she arched up and back as she pistoned like a rider on a bucking bronco. He pumped into her with deeper and faster strokes. Her thighs descended with increasing force, as if each time she were collapsing on the downward surge—only to revive just in time to draw her plundered belly up on his erection yet again . . . and again . . .

Fargo, tensing upward, felt the gripping of her loins as he penetrated her to the hilt. And her passage kept squeezing, milking, until he felt himself bursting, spurting far up into her, while her face contorted and twisted in her own fiery orgasm.

Then with a deep sigh, Amity crouched, limp and satisfied, over Fargo. Slowly, sighing contentedly, she eased off his passive body and moved up slightly to stretch languidly beside him. Soon she stirred and caressed his cheek, while Fargo told her some of his suspicions and ideas what might be done about them. Finally her questions were through and he was recovered, and restless, he slid from the bed.

"Guess I should say thanks, Skye. Well, I do say it," she murmured, watching him dress. He came over and gave her a kiss, then stood back and smiled.

"Thank me when this is all over, Amity. Right now I'd like to stay, but I got to have a quiet look around and then clear out. I'll ride back about nine o'clock." He walked to the window, then paused as he was about to slide out on the sill. "Wait, one more thing. Did you see any riders coming over the pass?"

"No."

"Any hoofprints, except those left by the wild band?"

"No," she answered slowly. "I'm sure if a shod horse had been on the trail I'd have noticed the shoe print in the snow."

"That's all. And, Amity—don't worry. Things are going to come out all right, though hell might pop before it's over with."

After climbing down the ladder, Fargo returned it to Zerbe's barn. Beginning there, Fargo went from barn to barn, examining the horses in each. There were five horses in Vern Koehler's barn. Two were his own, and the remainder were animals left to be shod. A powerful stallion Fargo had heard Koehler call Jerry caught his interest. The animal betrayed nervousness as Fargo fussed around his head.

Fargo returned to his own horse, waited until the sun had been up an hour, then pulled off two of the Ovaro's shoes. He rode directly to the blacksmith shop, tied his horse outside, then pounded heavily on Koehler's door.

"Whatcha want?" the blacksmith growled, "raising the dead this time o' day."

"Morning's half gone," Fargo answered cheerily. "My horse threw a shoe. If you don't feel like putting it back on again, I will."

Sleepy and surly, the blacksmith appeared. "I'll shoe your critter, but you hang around. It might fancy to take a bit outta me, then there'd be trouble."

While Koehler was putting on the shoe, Fargo remarked, "I think you're right about Mooch Paulson and where he got his poke. Wish I could have got him, but he knows more about this country than I do. He can't stay out there forever, though, and I'll be back. How's the man he stabbed?"

"You mean McHenry? Oh, Gil's still in bed, but he'll live," Koehler answered. "Live to get Moose Paulson if you don't."

It was then that Amity appeared. Desperate, she told Fargo that the hotel safe had been robbed and Modoc was being held and was asking for him. She acted her part well, and Fargo managed to appear astonished.

"Are you going back?" Amity asked anxiously.

"I did plan to finish paying my respects to Mooch Paulson, but I guess that can wait," Fargo explained. "I'll stop at Zerbe's for a meal, and then we'll light out for Lewiston."

Amity couldn't eat much. As for Fargo, he wolfed down six eggs, a beefsteak, some flapjacks, and five cups of coffee while carrying on an amiable conversation.

"You aren't human," she said reproachfully. "How can you eat at a time like this?"

"I'm hungry."

After breakfast he settled the bill, while she saddled up, and drew Zerbe aside. "I rode in with how many horses?"

"Three. Your pinto and two packs."

"Wrong. One horse, only the pinto. Don't know about those two, don't care to, but perhaps they belong to somebody someplace a goodly ways away."

"Why, I'm beholden to you for setting me straight."

"I'll count on that. I'll be back, maybe sooner than you think." Fargo then thanked Zerbe and left. Damrow's and Trent's mounts would vanish within hours, he bet, leaving no trace to tip off Hi Pockets about his boys' fate. Spring thaw would alert him soon enough. The trader had smarts, and he had the power and good reputation to win a indirect confrontation. He'd outsmart Fargo maybe, but he was maybe too smart by half and could outsmart himself easiest of anyone.

As Amity rode stirrup to stirrup out of the settlement, Fargo felt eyes on him, smug eyes mocking his stupidity. As soon as they were screened by brush, he told Amity to go on alone. "Keep riding, don't stop until you get to Modoc. Don't tell anyone that I may be coming back with your dust."

"Oh, if you could," she said fervently. "Do you think then you can show these men proof that Modoc wasn't in on the safe robberies?"

Fargo shrugged. "If Modoc wanted to hit Hi Pockets', he was in the place enough to know when the safe was fat. My horse was used to set him up. Your gold he could've grabbed anytime, and he would've cracked the hotel safe when he'd have an alibi, surely." But, Fargo thought, that didn't mean he thought Modoc innocent of other raps. He leaned forward, kissing Amity, his hand lingering on her shoulder a moment. "Now, get going. And no matter what you hear or see, don't come back."

He turned his horse and kept it to the brush until he was at the rear of the blacksmith shop. Crossing quickly to the shop, a chilly, deadly excitement ran through him. Vern Koehler's back was thirty feet away, and off to one side was a brown-haired man with a scarred upper lip. Fargo unholstered his revolver as he walked in without knocking.

"Right. Now, you get me the express pack and get me Amity's gold," he demanded, watching the men's reactions carefully.

Vern Koehler caught up a sawed-off shotgun,

whirled, and crouched in a single movement while the other man clawed for his holstered revolver.

"Try," Fargo said.

Koehler's hand dropped. "Okay, what's the game? A holdup?"

Fargo grinned metallically, glancing at the other. "Shuck your gun."

Cautiously the man unbuckled his gunbelt, while Koehler said to Fargo, "You're crazy, y'know. I didn't have anything to do with any robbery. Hell, man, I was here when the hotel safe got robbed. Gil McHenry will vouch for me, won't you, Gil? We was over talking about the cut Mooch gave you."

"Hell, Koehler," Fargo retorted, "I had a hunch you might know something about the first robbery when I came into Excelsior. In the first place, the day we talked about it down at Lewiston you stood near my horse unconcerned, unworried you'd get bitten. You're a blacksmith and have a way with horses; you understand them. You couldn't have known my horse wouldn't nip you unless you'd already had contact with it. So, if Modoc Thorne didn't ride my horse, then that leaves only you."

"Prove it!" Koehler sneered.

"Another thing. Paulson slipped. He played me for a sucker and built a fire, thinking I'd close in on him. If his escape was on the level, he'd never have betrayed his location with a fire. There was only one other answer. It was a smoke signal to you that I wasn't in Excelsior and the way was clear."

McHenry cut in doggedly, "Vern was never out of Excelsior."

"His horse Jerry was," Fargo retorted. "And that horse brought a heavy load over Diablo Pass, no doubt, like it was the first robber. There was proof of that."

"Study his shoes, then see if you can find a print between here and Lewiston," Koehler challenged.

Fargo grinned. "You mentioned that before, so I'd suspect Modoc Thorne, a hostler. You probably yanked Jerry's shoes off when you pulled a job, then put 'em on again as soon as it was finished. You almost managed it, but you left a sign along the way.

"Sign? What sign? I never left no sign in my life!"

"If was a splash of red on white snow," Fargo answered. "I knew high altitudes can start a man's or a horse's nose to bleeding, and I knew the wild horses probably could stand it without trouble. So when I found blood on the snow it looked like someone had driven a horse over the trail with a heavy load on its back. I went through the barns and examined every horse's nostrils. I found dried blood on Jerry's."

"You're making a mistake," McHenry started again. "Why, we— "

"Cork it," Koehler snapped. "He ain't got nothing, so don't talk, don't give him nothing."

"In a way you're right," Fargo said, grinning at McHenry. "Y'know, for somebody who was in bed earlier, you managed a great recovery."

"Hey, it wasn't all that bad. Mooch slashed my stomach, and it bled a lot, but it didn't go very deep."

"Let's see your bandage." Fargo's grin broadened, but it still failed to temper the cold steel in his eyes as McHenry failed to reply. "The easy way or the hard way, McHenry?"

McHenry looked less adamant, but his tone was even. "Piss it out your ear."

Fargo, training his revolver on Koehler, closed in and punched McHenry in the face. McHenry reeled against a support, doubling over. Fargo crowded him and struck a second time, feeling bone crunch against his fist. McHenry was bleeding at the mouth as he hit the dirt floor hard, flopping over.

Fargo grabbed McHenry's shirt and tore as he yanked upward. Then Fargo ripped aside the bandages across his stomach. The flesh was unmarked.

Fargo glared at McHenry. "No more bullshit. Nothing now but talk."

"Aw ri', aw ri', lay off, will you?" McHenry spluttered through his mashed lips. He rolled over, head down, coughing for breath while Fargo stepped back. And Koehler did something stupid. Whether he reacted out of panic, or hoping to help McHenry, or figuring to shut him up, it was immaterial; the point was, he dove for his shotgun.

Fargo saw Koehler's shotgun sweep upward. Quickly he swung his revolver and fired, all in one blur of motion. The two shots seemed to come in one drumroll of sound, the shotgun thunder overwhelming the crack of a revolver shot. But Fargo's shot exploded a fraction of a second before Koehler's.

Buckshot blew a hole in the roofing above, Koehler's aim thrown awry when he was drilled through the right pectoral muscle and pitched backward. Fargo ducked reflexively, already swiveling in a low crouch to confront McHenry—who was plunging, grabbing his own weapon. Fargo fired only to wound—and missed. McHenry made a quirking maneuver in the last split instant while he dropped the hammer on an answering shot. His bullet flicked Fargo's shirt on the inside of the arm, close by the armpit; it caused a slight nerve twitch while Fargo was aiming, triggering . . . and instead of the Colt .45 stunning McHenry, as Fargo intended, the slug punched into the center of his breastbone.

McHenry jerked, shuddering, and crumpled instantly, dropping his revolver and rolling onto one side, mouth agape, blood pulsing from his chest. Fargo took a step toward him, hearing the groan of air escaping his lungs. Then he heard a distant rush of voices and running feet, and then, much closer, the sharp blast of a bullet through the spot where he'd just been.

Pivoting, Fargo saw Koehler rising by some powerful drive of will, glassy-eyed, dark blood drenching his shirt. Fargo flung himself to the right as Koehler tottered at him, firing wildly. Propped on one elbow, Fargo sent a slug, again hoping to cripple, not to kill. Koehler ran smack into the bullet and seemed to go suddenly blind and crazy, a whirling dervish that fell flat on his face and expired.

Cursing his luck, wishing he had more answers now, Fargo glanced around at the carnage as alarmed locals rushed inside, some with weapons and all with outrage, wondering what the hell was going on.

11

Skye Fargo was lounging casually against the anvil block, revolver holstered, as men kept crowding inside, gaping and railing angrily. He remained calm and confident, refusing to answer much or argue less until Zerbe arrived. .

And then Fargo told them.

McHenry's lack of a knife wound helped his case. So did Zerbe's suggesting they search the place thoroughly, which convinced them when the boodle from both safe robberies was found, dug out of the coal in Koehler's forge and from under the hay in Jerry's manger. No hassles after that. It wasn't that Excelsior men had grown soft, only smart. Koehler, McHenry, and Paulson had been renegades, not sharing the risks or the rewards with the community, so they weren't worth defending.

Five horses, taken from Koehler and McHenry's stocks, were loaded with loot. Almost everything taken appeared recovered. Amity's trunk was full as ever, and Chilton's pack was only missing the gold poke, swiped by Pearson to use for boozing.

Over a trail packed hard by the wild horse herd, Fargo's train moved at a steady plod. He passed the scenes of violence with Damrow and with Trent. Fargo recalled his surprise that they had been after

Joel Dumas's ring. Why so much ado over one solitary ring, and especially a ring that was worth no more than ten dollars?

Moving on up through Diablo Pass, his practiced eye saw where Jerry, with the burden of the hotel-safe loot on his back, had gone deep into the snow at times. And Fargo noticed that Jerry's hoofs were unshod, though back in the barn he was wearing shoes now. Fitting Jerry with shoes was probably the first thing Koehler had done on this return from his raids. And it was no doubt this same Jerry that had stood in the river pool while Koehler, McHenry, and Paulson loaded the sway from Hi Pocket's safe onto his back.

Considering Fargo had left Excelsior in late morning, and the natural slowness of a packhorse string, he was gratified when he rode into Lewiston around nine in the evening. Leading the string down the middle of the street, Fargo attracted attention and so did his cargo, and a group began to collect around him when he drew in by the hotel. After giving his string a careful eye, to see if they hurt or needed tending at once—they didn't—Fargo went into the hotel. The lobby was cleaned but displayed the damages of the explosion. The safe itself was boarded over and the fat woman still slumped, snoring, a gauze-bandage turban around her head, an old octagonal-barrel shotgun across her lap.

Amity opened the door to his knock and ushered him in. "Modoc's still held. Nothing's changed, really," she reported fretfully. "And you?"

"I have the loot, almost all of it. All your dust, anyway."

She hugged him, clinging, kissing him hard. Breaking her impetuous embrace, Amity smiled up at Fargo. "Where is it?"

"On a packhorse outside." Grinning, he eased Amity from another clenching press, explaining, "Later, okay? I wanted to check with you, iron out a few things, but I can't stay. I got to tend the string and make sure nobody steals the stuff again."

She cast him a lidded glance. "I'll hold you to it."

"Great. Now, you want me to take the gold out? If so, you'll trust your gold to me from now on; no bossing, no complaining, no second guessing."

"I—I suppose, but where're you taking it out to?"

"Wallula. Close to a hundred miles away, but by pushing some, I should be there by midnight on the day following. If you can get Joel sobered up, you two can start a couple of days behind me, after I'm already in Wallula with your dust. You can take a Columbia River steamer to Portland and be fine."

Amity nodded. "I'd like Modoc to hear it. I do hope he's freed soon."

A heavy tread sounded in the hall, then someone tried the door. "It's Joel," Amity said, frowning, and went to unlock the door.

Joel Dumas lurched inside, not quite sober. He glanced indifferently at Fargo—and glanced again, flustered, his eyes wide with fear and awe. Then he stared at his sister for a long moment, scowling.

"Listen, Sis, I changed my mind. I was dumb to let you talk me into selling the claim, but I'll find another. I'm going to have me a hundred thousand bucks. A million!"

"Go to bed, Joel," Amity said wearily.

"The devil with that. I'm in a game, I need some more money."

Amity's voice was commanding. "If you spent your day's allowance, you're through for the day." Though she was probably only a couple of years older, it was apparent she was used to dominating him.

Joel turned, muttering, and clumped out and down the hall.

Amity gave Fargo a dry smile. "Now you see why it's difficult."

"I hope when his paint is rubbed off, you find sound wood underneath." Fargo turned toward the door, then glanced back, raking a hand through his hair. "You realize, Amity, even if you don't have the dust, I think you better wait two, three days, then drop a hint to Hi Pockets your dust slipped out." With a parting g'night, Fargo went out and shut the door after him.

The growing crowd was still around his string, and quietly watched him angle across the street toward the trading post. It was fairly crowded, a lot of comings and goings at the door, and as Fargo worked slowly through the crush, he heard snatches of conversation:

". . . got a swell ring for Maisy, Bill—a real diamond."

"Me, I got two for Delores, and two for myself. I ain't no cheapskate, I ain't."

Fargo glanced toward the two men, but the flow had already pushed them outside. Gazing around, he chanced to spot Joel Dumas seated at cards with his back to Fargo. Hi Pockets was in his usual corner with his safe and scales, and Fargo started his way back to him, flashing a great smile when Hi Pockets chanced to look his way. Hi Pockets stiffened, eyes bulging for all of fifteen seconds, and then he oozed into his genial demeanor.

"You sick?" Fargo asked at the counter. "Look peaked for a moment."

"Fighting a cold," Hi Pockets replied, choking. "Ain't seen you in a coupla or three days, now. Where you been?"

"Excelsior. But you already know that, you told Miss Dumas." Fargo waved negligently, adding, "No matter, I got two packhorses outside carrying the crap stolen from your safe."

"Strike me afire!" Hi Pockets grinned, showing yellow teeth, and shouted for others to gather around, he had news, fabulous news. That meant Fargo had to explain an edited, slightly fudged account. And when he was through, Hi Pockets declared, "Ain't surprisin', up in Excelsior. But you done more than most badge-toters ever lived to brag about. I dunno how to repay you, Skye."

"Don't weep, is one. Other is, free Thorne."

"Me? Why me? I'm not involved in that in any way."

"Maybe you weren't involved . . ." Fargo narrowed his eyes, struggling for control, his instincts urging him to erupt in anger. He hated pussyfooting no matter how necessary. But it was. "But you damn well better be as of now."

"Whoa up, Sky. I'll do what I can do, but we ain't all hard salts like you. You going after Mooch Paulson again?"

"Fuck Mooch Paulson. You want him, you get him."

A man at the bar suddenly called to Fargo, "Your lingo's offensive, mister!" He was sandy-haired, with a lined face and a mouth full of a long, newly lit torpedo cigar, but otherwise he was ordinary in looks and garb. And he was leaning on his left elbow, facing Fargo, his right hand hanging close to the pearl handle of a .44 Colt."

Fargo cupped his ear as though hard of hearing. "What?"

"You heard me, you heathen toad! Wash your mouth out."

Fargo stepped closer, frowning, cupping his ear. "What?"

"Wash your mouth out and ears out with soap!" the man yelled.

Fargo knew he was in for it. Washing his mouth out wouldn't be the end of the man's play, but merely the lead-up. He turned to Hi Pockets, asking, "Who's the parson?"

"Lang. New fellow, in for Nehalem."

"Where's Nehalem?"

"Left this morning for his Walla Walla office. Don't know when he'll be back."

Fargo had to smirk at the irony. Nehalem's being out of town at the time of an attempted killing was an old ruse to show he'd no connection. But of all places for the man to go visiting when Fargo and Amity were escaping. In a sense he was lucky, for at least he was forewarned and forearmed.

"You got two minutes, mister." Lang said. "I'll learn you decency and respect."

Fargo closed a few steps, cupping his ear. "You're learning wha'?"

Lang stepped clear of the bar. The area around them was clearing rapidly, the post emptying, and Hi Pockets shouted, "Why not take it outside, boys? I run a legit place."

"Shut up, Hi Pockets," Fargo told him without changing directions.

"Time's going, mister, and I don't see no soap," Lang called, dribbling smoke from his cigar. Fargo was gradually closing the distance, cupping his ear, making no move toward his gun. The man took a step back, trying to regain needed distance, but he bumped against the bar.

"Now, what were you saying?" Fargo asked amiably, pressing him back.

"Get off'n me, you shitfaced—!"

Still grinning, Fargo spanked the cigar, knocking it from Lang's mouth. At the same time his left hand darted forward, ripped Lang's pearl-handled pistol from its holster, and tossed it spinning behind the bar.

"Why—damn you!" Lang choked in amazement. He lashed out with his right hand at Fargo's face, the thick knuckles grazing Fargo's beard.

Swaying with the punch, Fargo slugged his own right into Lang's stomach, catching him just at the break of the ribs. He heard wind burst from Lang's lungs, and then he pistoned lefts and rights, driving the gunman against the bar.

Somewhere someone yelled, "Fight!"

Lang tried to counter, but that first punch to the wind had weakened him considerably. He hit Fargo in the gut with a right, but Fargo disregarded the blow. He set himself and rammed more one-two combinations into Lang's battered face, forcing the man backward along the bar. Drinkers hastily scurried out of range as Lang lurched toward them, blood streaming from his cut mouth and nose, eyes wild but swollen half shut. He swung a wild punch at Fargo's head, missed, and then collapsed suddenly when Fargo hit him in the stomach again, in the exact same spot.

A crowd had gathered around the fighters, but Fargo bulled his way through, having too much to do to waste any more time here. He paused near the door to glance back at Hi Pockets, and said in a loud, sharp voice, "Don't forget, you're going to do all you can to free Modoc. I don't want any more misunderstandings. Folks might get hurt."

He turned for the door again, and was heading outside when he heard the flattened, enraged Lang howl, "I'll blast your head clean off!"

Fargo gave a loud, scornful laugh as he walked out. The cluster was still growing across by the packhorses. He glimpsed a man who'd left just ahead of him running down the street to spread the news of the fight. Nearby, Joel Dumas was walking very fast, which made him appear furtive and silly. He was heading for the hotel. Fargo suspected he was harmless, but Joel's awkward stride implied inner turmoil—and possible danger.

Through the lobby-door window, he saw Joel going upstairs, flanked by two burly miners, a room key in hand, though he was registered in Room Six downstairs. Curious now, Fargo trailed after them and reached the second floor. He found the hallway empty. He padded along the hall, trying to avoid loose, creaky boards while keeping alert for sounds through the thin panels of doors. Abruptly he paused, hearing voices just ahead. Easing up to it, Fargo saw a small card, like a business or banker's card, tacked to the door:

THE LEWISTON JEWELER

Keeping his eye on the span of hall doors and the landing, Fargo strained to make sense of the muffled talk. After a few moments the door opened and the two miners brushed out, eyeing Fargo. Fargo eyed them back, shoving inside to cover his eavesdropping, and shut the door. Only Joel was there now, and he was bending over the bedcovers, tidying jewelry display trays.

Fargo leaned back against the door and shot home the bolt.

Joel straightened. Color drained from his face.

Fargo crossed slowly to the bed and stood spread-legged with his hands thrust deep in the pockets of his mackinaw. His keen blue eyes cut into Joel like points of steel, and the muscle lumps at either corner of his mouth were hard as rock. "I want to buy a ring, Dumas. A good one—say, about two hundred dollars."

There were trays holding rings and pendants and bracelets.

"Show me your prize collection," Fargo demanded.

Joel trembled like a leaf in the wind, perspiration beginning to bead his forehead. With palsied hands he reached into the case and set a tray of sparkling rings on the wooden counter.

"Give me your loup," Fargo pursued ominously.

"I—I ain't got a glass."

"Haven't you?" Fargo's hand came out of his pocket gripping his revolver.

Joel fumbled in the top bureau drawer and passed a small eyeglass. Quickly Fargo examined a few rings, then flipped the glass back to Joel and chuckled bitterly.

"So that's your game, eh?" he snapped. "Swindling these poor saps who don't know what to do with their gold."

A customer was rapping on the door. Glancing at it, Joel seemed to gain defiance from it. "Naw, they're satisfied, and I need the money, you seen how cheap my sis is. Besides, Hi Pockets is backing me and—"

"Hi Pockets would toss you to the wolves," Fargo scoffed angrily. "You got any proof? You do, he'll say he backed you thinking the jewels were real. I bet you don't. He'd deny it, and who'd take your word against his?"

Slumping, Joel sat down on the bed.

"You turn into enough of a pest, Joel, he'll waylay you with Damrow and Trent."

Jerking, Joel glanced up, his face pale. "I didn't, I don't know—"

"I'm no ghost, Joel. My body's not down in a blind ravine. I slipped and fell, instead of dropped," Fargo snarled. "Why did he want me dead? And don't lie and try to tell me it's nothing to do with the ring you gave me. I know it is."

"It ain't my fault. Hi Pockets makes it out like it is, like it wasn't my glass to bet and lose," Joel said truculently. "He remembered you from times before, that you knew stones. He feared you might drop remarks around its real value. We only now started and he didn't want to lose his investment."

Another customer began knocking, then thumping.

"Joel," Fargo warned. "Lock up and stay locked, you hear me?"

"Yes," Joel said truculently, sitting down on the bed.

Fargo nodded. "Remember this. Hi Pockets tried to kill me, he'd try to kill you. Tread lightly, but no more business. If I tell what I know, which I'm apt to do, ten to one, you'll swing at rope's end." He turned, walked to the door, unbolted it, and strode through the four men waiting to buy.

Returning to his string, Fargo began unloading the hotel safe loot. Most bystanders immediately helped out, carrying the loot inside to the fat woman. Then Fargo moved down to the post, and again bystanders unloaded those packs under Hi Pockets' scrupulous eye. With only the pack and Amity's gold aboard, Fargo took the string down to Thorne's livery and tended to the horses.

An hour later Fargo was almost finished when Modoc Thorne arrived.

"When I want my poker playing interrupted, I'll ask," Thorne said in mock anger. "I was plucking those fools at the jail like hens.

"They threw you out for cheating," Fargo retorted, and Modoc winked, jiggling his bulging pockets of loose change. "You better plan to stay up all night," The Trailsman said. "I didn't want to scare Amity, but a few two-legged coyotes may come around. I don't know if Hi Pockets knows Amity's dust is here, but he knows I am, and he feels he's got reason to shut me up for keeps."

Modoc nodded. "Yeah. I'll squat here by the door while you get some sleep. You'll have a hard day tomorrow, and I can snooze then."

"Well, I'll be a mite busy between now and daybreak, so I'll be awake to cover here. Might go for Amity, but if you could do a little spying on what's happening, you might get forewarning of a raid, and we'll be prepared." Seeing Modoc's affirmative nodding, Fargo asked, "Your gun working good?"

"Dunno. It's a woodworking gun I carved as a kid, and never tried to fire it," he fibbed. "You got a good notion there, Skye. I'll keep my ears to the ground and my nose to the grindstone, but it's a bad position to fight in."

After Modoc left the barn, Fargo completed his tending. Then he lit a number of lanterns that he hung in a high, brightly illuminated space, and then set to work. Cold breezes whistled through the cracks. Noises from the trading post filtered in on occasion. Fargo worked patiently, wanting to be finished by dawn, and managed to complete it with a few hours to spare.

He ate a cold snack, and made another thorough check around the barn as a precaution. He was almost done, coming around from the front double doors, when the door of the little stable office opened and the glow of a hand lantern spilled inside. Fargo wheeled back against the wall, his revolver whipping up in his right hand; his eyes turned a brutal ice-blue.

Half through the door, Amity Dumas saw him, saw his gun. Shock widened her eyes. She stopped bolt still, gasping. Fargo grunted and slid his revolver smoothly into its holster, then took a deep breath of relief.

Coming over, Amity asked, "Do you always jump at shadows?"

"On occasion, shadows have taken potshots my way."

"It can't be very nice, suspecting anything that moves behind your back."

"I quit expecting life to be nice when I was eight," Fargo replied, and gave an easy grin. "Never mind me. What're you here for?"

"Holding you to your word, remember?" She came up to him and took him by the arm. "Can we try it in some hay?"

Fargo laughed, and started down the aisle toward the smallish mound of dry hay. "What's your game, anyway?"

She gazed at him, studying him as though unsure he wasn't playing her for a fool, and reaching the haystack, she said, "I thought it was very obvious. You arouse me like no man has done, maybe because you're more animal than most, or maybe because I'll have to be civilized after this." Then she laughed delightedly, and began flinging her clothes off.

Stripping buff naked, Fargo and Amity lowered onto the hay. She gasped with pleasure, her body undulating in response to his hands while he massaged her flesh to yearning arousal again. Fargo positioned himself over her, feeling her thighs widen to cradle him, her ankles locked around his calves as he pressed down on her loins, inserting himself firmly.

Thus entwined, they began the simple yet urgent flexing of buttocks, hardening and softening of the muscles, a gentle rocking of one body impaled by another. Amity breathed raggedly, her lips drawn down slightly, the right corner of her mouth twitching as passions coursed up between her clasping thighs. Fargo lowered his head and their mouths fused together, their tongues touching and flicking in play. Fargo began to plunge deeper and more swiftly.

Amity shuddered and moaned, and he quickened to a violent thrusting. Their bellies slapped together. Amity quivered with each sliding jolt, grinding against him as her orgasm neared. Abruptly she cried out in release, high-pitched sounds of wanton ecstasy. Clenching his teeth, Fargo felt his orgasm welling up, flowing deep inside her, flooding her. She splayed her legs wide, arching up with pressing force to hold the last bits of joy there between her legs.

Slowly Fargo settled down on her soft, warm body. He lay, crushing her breasts and belly with his weight, until his immediate sensation began to wane. Finally he eased off her passive body, slid away to extinguish the lamps, and moved back to burrow under the hay, cozy warm . . . but only for a minute, he told himself. Only a minute.

They dozed off before they realized it, their bodies gently entwined.

12

It was still dark when Skye Fargo awoke, alert as a cougar. A sound had grated—the stir of boots or the whispered creak of a hinge. Here we go again, Fargo thought as he reached for the revolver and cocked it.

From the barn's darkness came a man's careful breathing, then the words: "Easy, Skye. It's Modoc."

Fargo sat up. "Hell of a joint you run," he observed, yawning, as Thorne scratched a match, lit one of the lanterns, and approached. "No privacy at all."

"It's liable to get worse." Thorne grinned at Amity. "I might've known."

"Why, you old goat, you've been trying to get me on your feed sacks all along," she retorted, buried modestly in the hay. "What's wrong?"

"Hi Pockets is up to something. Meeting with some of his boys, talking up law'n order. The more he's pious, the worse he is."

Fargo said, "Maybe a gun barrel rammed between that gent's teeth will change his mind for him."

"Too late. He's surrounded by a crew of hardcases." He started back toward the door, pausing once to glance back and add, "You better not fiddle around. Get going to Wallula."

Fargo was first up, tossing Amity her garments. They had barely finished when Fargo straightened, muscles tightening, as a gun exploded just outside.

"Stay here," he snapped at Amity, racing in that direction. A gun fired again, and was answered by two guns or one firing fast. In a crouching run Fargo sped through the little door, seeing in the dimness the form of Modoc behind a large water trough. Fargo crawled up.

"Who is it, Modoc?"

"How do I know?" Thorne fired again. "Caught 'em with their britches down, thinking they was making an easy sneak on you. Watch yourself. They're in that brush over there. Only a couple, I think."

The brushy flat ahead ran down to the creek. The prowlers had taken cover close to each other and probably still believed they had but one man to contend with, a circumstance Fargo meant to exploit. He held his fire, and for a long moment there was a hushed, taut stillness.

Thorne shattered the silence, with two crimson flashes coming in instant response. At an angle from Modoc, Fargo laid down his fire, triggering fast. There was a yelp and, a moment later, the sound of pounding feet.

"That sure spooked 'em," Modoc grunted. "And I reckon you plugged one."

Prospecting carefully, they found the man in the small clump of brush that had failed to give him much protection. Fargo rolled him over, but couldn't identify him, although the guy had an ugly face not easily forgotten.

"Roarke Keats," Modoc said. "Haven't seen him around for ages, but he used to run with Damrow and Trent, and they all work for Hi Pockets."

"Worked. They all worked for Hi Pockets."

"Do tell. I thought Damrow and Trent were scarce lately." They started to walk carefully around the outside of the barn, the same way Fargo had checked the interior, and presently Modoc said, "This makes a difference, Skye. We've crippled Hi Pockets' organization by killing those three. Maybe we've cut them off from that outlaw gang. If that's the case, we've got Hi Pockets in a spot where he'll have to take the field itself."

"You mean, if we shove out all the bait we can scrape up."

Modoc scratched his scalp. "What do you mean."

"We've got two kinds of bait. He wants back what he lavished on Amity and he's got a reason or two to come after me. If we all head for Wallula together it'd be just as safe for the Dumases, and maybe we can force Hi Pockets into making one big play. If we can beat him, we won't have to worry about those two-bit wolves he pays off."

"Danged if I don't think you're right, Skye. And I'll come along as far as Wallula myself."

Fargo gazed at Modoc Thorne, thinking: fair enough. Somewhere along the run the story of that attack on the ridge would come out . . .

When dawn came, they built a fire and fixed breakfast, and when they had eaten, Fargo said, "I'll wait here another hour while you two go get Joel up and ready. Instead of trying to sneak out of the country, we'll whoop it up."

An hour later, Fargo drove his horse string down the main street of the raw mining settlement with considerable clatter and shouting and spraying snow. Amity was asaddle her favorite mount from the livery, a red roan, leggy and tough. Joel was wavering aboard a splotch paint, which more or less resembled its rider's appearance. Modoc was on a roman-nosed gelding that looked to be a deep-chested, dependable brute. He also had a good stock saddle, a Winchester and saddle holster and a warbag, and a bridle trimmed in silver conchas. Fargo doubted there was a person in Lewiston left unaware of their pullout.

The dirty gray of tents slid past, and the racket of searching men behind faded out. Ahead lay all of a hundred miles of rough trail to cover before they reached Wallula, more than they could put behind them in a single day, rough outlaw trail offering unending chances for bushwhackers. As the day lightened, the mountains sunk against the horizon behind them, and they were working doggedly across the snow-laden sagebrush plain that lay between the Blue Hills and the Snake.

Fargo was jogging along in deep preoccupation, the string filing up in a long, gentle slant, when the beat of hoofs on the trail behind swiveled him in the saddle. Fingers resting on the stock of his Sharps, he saw a rider tear around the bend below, coming fast. Fargo was still halted, startled when Hi Pockets pounded up.

Hi Pockets smiled disarmingly. "Why so nervous?" he demanded affably.

The train had kept moving, the other saddle passengers with it, yet Fargo sat still for another moment. "What's the idea, Hi Pockets? Where are you heading?"

"Wallula, if you must know. Business. I hurried a

little, hoping I could enjoy your company." And Hi Pockets' rosy face beamed amiably.

The bland, almost sneering pretense irritated Fargo, but he wasn't ready to make an issue of it yet. Then, as he wheeled around and gigged his mount to overtake the pack string, he began to understand that perhaps an advantage or two might have tilted his way. He had cut off Hi Pockets' contact with the outlaw gang and left him little time for improvisations, forcing him into personal participation. It brought the man a long way out of his clever cover, yet the scheme behind this bold move was anything but clear.

Hi Pockets spurred on to join Thorne and the Dumases. That made him Thorne's problem to handle, which was okay by Fargo. Cunning and courageous as he may be, Hi Pockets could not hope to surprise and overcome four people already warned against him and feeling alert.

Hi Pockets' intentions grew clearer in the ensuing hours. At noon they made cold camp on Crow Hop Creek, pausing awhile to rest and graze the horses. By this time Joel Dumas had enlivened considerably and, passing close to him, Fargo caught the heavy whiff of whiskey. When he got a chance to speak to Modoc, Fargo asked, "That fool kid got a bottle?"

Modoc grinned sourly. "Hi Pockets gave it to him. Said he needed some dog hair."

"You mean brave-maker."

Modoc shook his head. "The kid's sound if he has a chance to come to his senses. I don't reckon he'll let his sister down, but Hi Pockets can sic him on us easy as hell." Glancing across at Joel and Hi Pockets, Modoc added, "That don't mean I ain't tempted to kick his fool breeches and gutshoot Hi Pockets."

"I'd settle for taking the bottle away from him," Fargo growled, "but it'd likely cause a showdown. If Hi Pockets tries to spark a quarrel, you and me're going to be the sweetest-dispositioned cusses this side of heaven."

Joel began to drink openly after a while. Amity, watching in disgust, did not interfere, either, seeming to realize that the situation was too ticklish for haggling. Fargo began to hope that Joel would eventually pass out, in which event he could be tied to a horse and kept out of trouble. Then, as Fargo was readying to hit the trail again, Joel came up to him, his bloodshot eyes hostile.

"Listen, Fargo, we don't have to poke along with this damned train. Sis says she turned our dust over to you. We'll take it and get along."

Fargo smiled at him. "To get it you'll have to get me."

"Don't hand me that guff no more. I fell for it once, you and your bad-mouthin', but not no more. I'll take bossing off Amity, but nobody else. You aren't telling me I can't handle my own dust."

"If your sister says the word I'll give you your share of it."

Joel stomped off and Fargo saw him talking angrily with Amity. Hi Pockets was watching this with seeming indifference. Presently the train was moving quietly along the trail again. Joel finished his bottle and smashed it against some rocks, giving Fargo some hope that in a few hours, Joel would be more sober and sensible. Shortly after four that afternoon, Hi Pockets dropped back to the end of the string. Fargo watched him with hard-eyed suspicion, but Hi Pockets made no effort to talk. A little later they crossed Thistle Creek, and abruptly Fargo reined in.

Swinging the Ovaro around, Fargo swooped down with one long arm and picked up a cloth from the side of the trail. He examined it, then handed it to Hi Pockets, saying. "Your kerchief. At least, it's got your initials."

Hi Pockets stared. "My initials, alright. But hardly my handkerchief."

"I saw you drop it. That's why I picked it up."

Hi Pockets smiled, then shrugged. "I grow more absentminded every day. If it's mine, thanks." He tucked the kerchief away and caught up with the Dumases.

Fargo watched them, worry throbbing in his mind. It was clear now that Hi Pockets expected to meet somebody out here. He had sent word. They would be coming down Thistle Creek, which followed a canyon out of a piece of wild country that would make an excellent bandit hangout. Hi Pockets had tried to tell his men which way to turn when they struck the main trail. No doubt he would manage to plant other signs.

Along toward evening, Fargo picked their campsite with great care, choosing a hilltop above a small, frigid creek, a spot within reach of potable water and grass under pawable snow, affording a fair view in all directions. Even so, he knew that if an attack was coming there was little that could be done to stave it off. He saw that Thorne looked worried, too, and he made opportunity to tell him how Hi Pockets had tried to mark their trail at Thistle Creek.

Thorne listened somberly. "It's Amity I'm worried about. We can't risk a gun ruckus. But by hell, if we do have trouble, he's the first man I'll plug."

"I've a notion how we might spike his guns. Modoc, you pick a squabble with that ninny Joel."

"That oughta be easy. Fun, too, and damn overdue." 🖉

Two horses had carried the camp supplies and bedrolls, with the rest carrying cargo like Amity's trunk and Chilton's express pack. While Fargo unpacked the gear, Thorne stomped over to Joel. "Git up off'n your dead ass, kid. We got camp to make, and you can do your share. Or are you too rich for that kind of work now?"

The reaction was instantaneous. Joel stared at him for a moment, his eyes kindling into a blaze of anger. "Damn you, git your snout out of my doings! I didn't invite myself on this gawdforsaken trip, but that's about all I'm taking of it. I'm inviting myself off!" He stomped over to Fargo, his fists on his hips. "No more shuffle, Fargo. Cough up that dust!"

Fargo shrugged indifferently. "Help yourself."

"Help myself where?"

"Where do you think?"

Joel pounced on the trunk, sneering till he opened it . . . and found it contained a skillet, coffeepot, and stew kettles. Then he started to search, rummaging through the cargo, then combing through the supplies, emptying utensils and dumping bags of foodstuffs and staples. He turned furiously to Fargo's bedroll.

"Stay out of my things," Fargo warned. "I catch you messing with them again, I'll shove you and your spilled guts in the nearest river."

"I didn't, I—" Joel stammered, squirming, reddening, patently admitting he ransacked Fargo's room. Fargo had tossed the line to see if anything bit, due to the similar style of trashing in his room and this train. He was right, but Joel Dumas rebounded belligerently. "Well, if it ain't in your stuff, where'd you cache it? You've been playing us for fools! I told Amity not to trust you, or that dog Thorne! Where's the dust?"

Fargo grinned and shrugged.

Staring with interest, Hi Pockets stalked forward. "Listen, Fargo, something's funny here. Impolite as it seems, I think we'll take a look in your pack." His pudgy hand made a surprisingly fast movement into his coat and emerged with a stubby derringer. Fargo shrugged, gave no resistance. Joel emptied out the Trailsman's personal effects, scattering them carelessly but finding nothing.

Joel's face was shocked and serious. "Sis, you know anything about this?"

"I don't understand it." Amity glanced with puzzlement at Fargo. "Did you change your plans?"

"I agreed to get you and your dust to Wallula. On my terms."

She smiled bitterly. "I guess I misplaced my trust, Joel. I should've listened to you. I expect the dust is still somewhere around Lewiston, and when we reach Wallula, we'll be told to wait there for it. And that'll be the last we'll see of it." She turned savagely to Thorne. "You're in it, too!"

Thorne scowled. "We work together on occasions."

"Well, we're heading back to camp ourselves, tomorrow morning," Joel snapped, swelling a bit in pride. "We're not letting this pair of jacklegs out of our sight until we have the dust."

Hi Pockets' eyes mirrored bafflement mixed with

suspicion. "Something's funny here," he growled again, mostly to himself.

It was a tight-nerved camp. While Thorne and Fargo went about their routines unconcerned, Hi Pockets and Joel retired for a long powwow. Amity came up to Fargo, smiling. "You've sure stumped the men Skye, but I trust you."

Fargo grinned back. "Hi Pockets' started a big ball rolling and now he's scared it's all for nothing. He likes a sure bet, and he won't risk his neck unless he's sure what he wants is here."

She looked at him pertly. "Well, is it?"

"It's safe. It's Hi Pockets' hide I'm after now."

Amity smiled softly and bent to lift the coffeepot off the fire.

Fargo had been rolled up in his blankets for two hours when he saw Hi Pockets rise cautiously behind the dying fire and make his stealthy way across the camp to disappear down the slope.

Fargo eased to Thorne and woke him. "Pockets just floated out."

Thorne sat up. "Which way's the toad going to jump, Skye?"

"I'd figured he went to call it off."

Fargo crossed to where the Dumases had spread their bedding and roused them. Amity was awake and up instantly, but Joel was deep in sleep. Fargo shook him roughly. "Some watchdog, kid. But you better have that gun handy now. Your fat friend's gone to meet a few of his friends."

A quarter of an hour passed before Hi Pockets returned. He skulked up the slant, hesitated a moment when he saw the entire camp was stirring, then came in boldly. "Dang me, it woke you all up too? Sounded worth checking. Only a horse scraping a rock, I guess."

Joel was frowning at Fargo. "What the hell were you up to?"

"I'm up to more sleep," Fargo said, yawning, but what he really wanted was quiet, so he could hear someone coming.

"Figure you can trick me and Amity up that easy?" Joel pressed, louder.

Fargo shrugged, glancing around as he started to turn from Joel. Hi Pockets was making an elaborate pretense of going to bed. Amity looked anxious, as she usually did around her brother, and Thorne began to say something about seeing how it looked in the morning, when Joel yelled, "Don't put your back to me, you yellow-livered skunk! It's just like Hi said, you're out to get me. You'd shoot me down like a dog if you could!"

Fargo turned to glare at Joel. "You are going to step over the line."

"Any time! I'll shoot you down like the sneakin' cur you—" He broke off, his startled gaze going to the edge of the clearing.

The others began turning to look as well, only to be checked by a purring, calm voice. "Don't move, my friends. If you do, you die very quick."

Fargo turned anyway. Four bearded men came walking in from the sides, revolvers in their fists. The biggest of them stalked straight toward Amity Dumas, placed a calloused hand on her slender neck, then turned to face Fargo. "Friend, you choose which we take, the gold or the gal. Both are nice."

Fargo stood immobile. Hi Pockets had crawled out of his blankets again, but Fargo could not see

160

his face. An explosive protest came from Joel, and Thorne swore under his breath.

"Mark it, Joel," Fargo said calmly. "How'd they know they'd have to force me to dig up the dust? A man might figure they'd been tipped off."

There was a tight moment's silence. "Why, damn you, Hi Pockets!" Joel yelped. "You had this fixed all the time!"

"Cut out your blasted yammering." Hi Pockets' eyes flashed. "You've been one of the most bungling nincompoops I've ever wasted a breath on."

"Easy," Fargo warned, then faced Hi Pockets and laughed. He sounded suddenly very amused. "You ought to know there's no gold. Never was any."

Hi Pockets' face hardened. "You tried that on me? A trap? A baited trap?"

Fargo grinned. "You guessed it, big man. I just didn't try it on you—I worked it on you."

The big outlaw thumbed the hammer of his revolver. "Where's the gold?"

Fargo, facing death, laughed. "You'll never know. And the laugh's on you," he chortled. "For a long time you been operating on a slick reputation. You ain't had to identify yourself with any of the dirty work once. You play it safe, just like you're trying to play this and aim to in the future. But y'see, we got the hole card. If these pals of yours try to take Miss Dumas, Modoc, me, or Joel'll gutshoot you. We can't miss. If they try to beef us first, one of us will surely get you in the shootout. I promise you that. How about it? You want to convict yourself in front of the four of us, or die?"

Fargo saw Hi Pockets' face whiten, and knew he had nailed the man to the quick and the true.

"Okay," Hi Pockets finally said, and turned to the big, bearded hombre. "Leave her and get out." He waited until the man had backed away, grumbling, then he started saying, "But you'll let me—" as suddenly he whirled, the derringer in his fist spitting flame.

Fargo had known that this had to come, that Hi Pockets did not dare leave the four of them alive now that he'd made his incriminating link. He was diving to the ground before the first shot. The acquiescence had been a cover, and now Hi Pockets heaved himself forward to get behind Amity.

Fargo couldn't help her right then, for one of the outlaws was shooting at him, the discharge almost blasting in his face, and he felt the slug rip across his shoulder as he left his feet, and then his head hit the big, bearded man in the middle and they went down in a tangle. Fargo twisted as he hit ground and, rolling, came around to catch another of the outlaws up through the stomach. That man was a little handicapped because he was afraid to shoot for fear of hitting the big, bearded fellow knotted with Fargo.

But Amity didn't need much help right then. She whirled, administering a stinging slap across Hi Pockets' face, cutting and racing away to give Fargo or Thorne clearance while the owlhoot bunch raised a ruckus of shots.

Hi Pockets picked Joel as his least dangerous foe, and he made a fatal mistake. Cool and suddenly mature, Joel slapped for his pistol and dropped the fat man two paces short of Amity. And Modoc Thorne, with a swiftness from naturally quick reflexes and practice, corkscrewed his revolver out in an arc and across his body as fast as Fargo had ever seen a man grab a gun. More gun-thunder hit, Fargo and Modoc dropping a man apiece in twin explosions. The last man turned to run, but Joel's barking pistol brought him down.

A vast quiet followed.

An hour later, the coffee was done. The interval had been unpleasant while the bodies were disposed of. Joel sat quietly, recovering from the shock of his first gun fray, reliving it in his thoughts.

"Hi Pockets, he figured I'd side with him when the shooting started. His mistake was threatening Sis." He sat quietly for a long moment, staring into the fire, then acknowledged glumly, "Boy, was I sure acting the bonehead."

"You'd a-fooled me," Fargo responded. "I didn't think you was acting."

The trek took longer than if Fargo had been pushing along alone, but they made respectable time, and eventually the pack train rolled into the river community of Wallula.

Wearily they drew up, dismounted, and straggled toward a restaurant across the street. Fargo wasn't looking as sharp as usual; Amity was alongside him, wheedling as she had since the gunfight to find out where Fargo had put the dust. And Fargo was playing her curiosity for all it was worth.

"You'll have to wait and see, Miss Dumas."

"But we're here now, Skye. No need to wait, I want to see!"

"All I'll say now is, it'd be a job for me to locate that dust myself. You nor Joel nor any sidewinder will find that gol—look out!"

All in a fleeting blur, Fargo had seen a buggy drawn by a pony slewing in front of them and the driver plying his whip. Behind the driver came a rider. Irked by the troublesome vehicle in front of him, the rider was trying to pass around. To do it he had to crowd Amity and Fargo, and he did so without so much as a howdy-do.

Fargo caught Amity in time to prevent her from toppling into the mud. Straightening her on wobbly legs, he stared after at the man's back and then at his boot, which a hoof had raked. "You go on ahead, have some food," he suggested to Amity. "I suddenly see an old friend of mine."

"I bet," Amity replied, wiping herself off. "Say hello for me, too."

Taking three long strides, Fargo had the bridle of the horse in his left fist. He looked down again to make sure, and saw the bruise that in healing had twisted his leg.

"Your horse?" Fargo asked softly.

"Mine," the man snapped. "Take your damn hands off!" He wore an ordinary rough coat, his jaws were plastered with a dark beard, and a drooping eyelid concealed half of his left eye. He jerked hard on the reins and then, Fargo's grip holding, recognition dawned in his face.

His reaction was immediate. His right hand brushed down and up again; gun metal gleamed at the end of his fist.

No sir, that would not do. Fargo jumped for the gun wrist as the man fired. Hot wadding peppered his neck, the bullet blasting harmlessly between his head and shoulder. Then with a twist of his wrist, Fargo yanked.

The rider came down on top of him. Tough-muscled as a bear, he caught a hand under Fargo's chin, closing down on his windpipe. They were rolling in the muddy snow of the street, with traffic shying away on all sides. His breath cut off, pinpoints of pain exploding in his brain, Fargo battled to hold the revolver. He heard a man's hoarse yelling, plus the rattle and grind of iron-shod wheels, but was boo busy to turn his head.

The pony drawing the buggy had spooked at the

shooting, slammed into a flapping tent front, and now was careening back down the way it had come. The driver sawed without effect on the lines. It was the gunman who saw what was coming. He let go of Fargo's throat and tried to scramble clear.

Fargo was starting up when the tornado hit him. A hoof cracked into his left shoulder, numbing the whole side of his body. He went down in a flurry of snow and muck and spattering hooves. He knew what was coming next and bunched up. The wheels straddled him in a flash and were gone. The buggy went over on its side with a splintering of wood.

Fargo crawled to his feet, reaching inside his coat. It was a wasted effort. The wheel that had missed him had lain open the gunman's head. One look was enough.

After the local doc had gone over Fargo for broken bones and given him a clean bill of health, Modoc Thorne insisted Fargo buy them all a round. "It's against God and nature to get run over by a horse and buggy without having something to show for it."

As Amity and Joel came up, Fargo said, "Okay, I'll tell you where your gold is. We'll have to rip up all the pack cushions to find it. I pulled some of the stuffing out of the padding and sewed your pokes up inside." Then, grinning, he very deliberately pulled out of his pocket a tattered strip of canvas. He matched it against Thorne's canvas coat.

Thorne grinned. "You looking for the place that came from? Take a look at that dead gunhawk's horse. He had canvas packs on the saddle and one of the flaps is ripped."

"Glad to hear it," Fargo said softly.

"So am I," replied Thorne. " 'Cause I figure you

and me have some time to spend together yet. The gold and letters you're packing for Chilton still have to get out of the area. There's honest men banking on you to do that, and I don't see any point in disappointing them. Thought I'd ride on a little farther with you and show you the land like a Thorne knows it. That is, if you're for it."

"Well, hell," the Trailsman grinned. "I guess I am. Now, where's that drink?"

LOOKING FORWARD!
The following is the opening
section from the next novel in the exciting
Trailsman series from Signet:

THE TRAILSMAN #75
COLORADO ROBBER

October 1861—in the highest and roughest
mining camps of Colorado Territory,
where winter threatens to arrive at any
moment, and greed and suspicion are
a way of life . . . and death.

Slate-gray clouds swirled ever lower, obliterating
the summits of the soaring mountains. What remained below was a dismal view of one of the many
mining camps in Colorado Territory.

They called it Buckskin Joe, after a swaggering
mountain man who had discovered gold a year ago.
Its raw ramshackle buildings pressed along one edge
of Buckskin Creek. Behind the single street rose a
steep, barren, rock-strewn slope.

Not all that long ago, it had been pristinely beautiful. Now it was riddled with fresh stumps and strewn with logging slash. The ground was pockmarked with prospect holes and scarred by the waste dumps of several mines. The precipitous slope rose several hundred feet before mercifully vanishing into the swirling dark fog.

For the past six October days those clouds had been blocking the accustomed warmth of the sun. Even worse, they formed an inexhaustible supply of drizzle. The stuff was too cold to be rain but too fluid to be snow. This wretched weather overpowered slickers and buffalo robes. It slithered beneath clothes and crawled into a man's sinews and bones. It made his muscles stiff, brittle, uncooperative.

So Skye Fargo was just as glad that, for a change, he wasn't out in it this morning. Five days of such misery outdoors, heading south for the winter after a trailing job in Montana, were more than enough.

This was a Belly Day. A day meant for lying indoors, belly-to-belly with a good warm woman. Outside, pellets of frigid moisture plunked harmlessly against the log cabin's shake-shingled roof. Indoors, coffee and stew simmered atop a radiant cast-iron stove. Two people managed to get even warmer atop the feather mattress that adorned a brass bedstead.

"Oh, Skye Fargo. There is so much of you. And yet I cannot get my fill."

Her words were spoken softly with just a trace of a Hungarian accent. The soft sounds came as a pleasant interruption to the tall, muscular man who'd been sitting up in bed, looking out the cabin's sole window.

The Trailsman shifted, exchanging the dismal view for one of the most exquisite faces he'd ever encountered. Her slender visage was framed by blond hair that tumbled in riotous curls to her shoulders, glowing like desert sunshine. When she smiled, which was often, her thin lips expanded and took on a ruby hue. Dimples appeared in her creamy cheeks. Above her pert nose, deep-set blue eyes sparkled with anticipation as she joined Fargo in sitting up.

For a moment, Fargo's eyes moved downward to savor her melonlike breasts. Each was crowned with a nipple that looked like a ripe wild cherry but tasted much sweeter. With a blush that spread from her face downward, she pulled a soft cotton bedsheet up to cover her scenery. She extended her right hand to knead Fargo's scarred shoulder.

Women were like that, he mused while enjoying the way her soft hand warmed and soothed his flesh. No matter how friendly they'd just been with a man, women always acted embarrassed and pulled something over themselves when they sat up. Perhaps that just added to the pleasure, since his lake-blue eyes moved back to her animated face while the sheet gave him something to slide his hands under.

Her smile grew even broader as Fargo's questing hands found her breasts beneath the thin sheet. He cupped each one, sliding his thumbs over the nipples. His fingers traced across the smooth skin. He increased the pressure while she responded in kind. The sheet forgotten, her left hand rose to Fargo's other shoulder and she pulled him toward her.

The big man paused only to sweep the sheet out of the way. Their tongues met for an extended, exuberant kiss. When he came up for air, he moved down, flicking at her neck before suckling her right nipple. When he moved to the left, she was in constant motion below him, arching up and down in a rhythm made audible by her hungry panting.

"Now, Skye, now," she urged. "Do not waste any more time."

Her taut legs spread to encircle Fargo's waist with dry warmth as he slid forward, his throbbing staff finding her warmth wet all on its own.

"Oh, that is right, that is so right," she murmured, unhooking her ankles and planting them on the mattress to give herself better leverage. Perhaps half as big as Fargo, she needed it in order to thrust upward and take in his plunges.

Automatically he reached for a pillow to put under her bobbing rear. She caught the motion and shook her head, curls flying. "It is better this way. You should not have to do all the work."

What they were doing didn't seem at all like work to the Trailsman, but the lady could use some help. He slid his hands from her breasts to her ribs, then around to the small of her back. Grasping a firm buttock with each hand, he began pulling her to him with each deepening stroke.

He was just about there when her knees came down. She extended each limb, then slowly sidled each leg so that it was wedged between Fargo and the mattress. Her action cost him some penetration as her legs came closer together. But her back continued to oscillate, her tight moist depths rising to meet each of Fargo's slowing thrusts.

"It feels so good," she breathed, "to have so much of you pressed against me. And I have already as much of you in me as I need."

Fargo liked the sensation of thighs against thighs, and just kept pushing. Her pale skin, growing pinker by the moment, provided visible evidence of what he could already feel with every nerve in his body—she was ready.

And so was he. . . .

RAY HOGAN KEEPS THE WEST WILD

☐ **THE DOOMSDAY MARSHAL AND THE HANGING JUDGE by Ray Hogan.** John Rye had only his two guns to protect the most hated man in the west. That's why he was picked to ride gun for the judge who strung up more men than any other judge. It's a twisting terror trail for Rye—from Arizona to Nebraska.   (151410—$2.75)

☐ **THE RAWHIDERS.** Forced outside the law, Matt Buckman had to shoot his way back in. Rescued from the savage Kiowas by four men who appeared suddenly to save him, Matt Buckman felt responsible for the death of one and vowed to ride in his place. Soon he discovered that filling the dead man's boots would not be easy . . . he was riding with a crew of killers . . . killers he owed his life to. . . .   (143922—$2.75)

☐ **THE MAN WHO KILLED THE MARSHAL.** He had to force justice from the law—at gunpoint. Dan Reneger had come to the settlement at the edge of nowhere to escape his gunslinging past. But he was in trouble from the start . . . in a town where the marshal knew his name.

(148193—$2.50)

☐ **THE HELL ROAD.** He was carrying a treacherous hostage and a million dollar coffin through a death trap! He was fair game for Indians, Confederates and bandits, but Marshak was the only man in the Union who could handle this impossible mission—all he had to do was survive.   (147863—$2.50)

Prices slightly higher in Canada.

**Buy them at your local
bookstore or use coupon
on next page for ordering.**

There's an epidemic with 27 million victims. And no visible symptoms.

It's an epidemic of people who can't read.

Believe it or not, 27 million Americans are functionally illiterate, about one adult in five.

The solution to this problem is you... when you join the fight against illiteracy. So call the Coalition for Literacy at toll-free 1-800-228-8813 and volunteer.

Volunteer Against Illiteracy.
The only degree you need is a degree of caring.